SAVING GAIA

CUTTER LAKEWOOD

Saving Gaia by Cutter Lakewood

ISBN 978-1-952027-10-9 (Paperback)
ISBN 978-1-952027-11-6 (Hardback)

New Leaf Media, LLC
175 S. 3rd Street, Suite 200
Columbus, OH 43215
www.thenewleafmedia.com

CHAPTER 1

In a small conference room off the main stage at the NY Hilton, Dr. John Loveton was preparing for his presentation for the United Nations Climate Conference. His wife Kate was concerned about the death threats he'd received since he went public with his findings and recommendations. Sitting at a conference table, she said, "Look, John I know how important this is to you, but let's look at the big picture. You can't save the world by yourself. John, not everyone sees things the way you do. You've stirred up a hornet's nest. I had to pull Tommy out of school. The forces against you are too powerful.

Let's take a look at what's happened John. You lost your research grants, you're on suspension from the university, and you are in danger of losing your tenure. And, the phone calls. Night and day, threats John, death threats against you. For Christ's sake, they killed our dog and ransacked the house. And for what? I'm begging you. Please. Please don't do this. If you won't do it for me, do it for Tommy. We can't survive this alone. Just look out the window at the angry protesters. The police are even wearing riot gear for Christ's sake."

John got up from the table and pacing back and forth said, "Kate, we've been over this a thousand times. I am doing this for you. For you and Tommy and everyone else on this godforsaken planet. If anyone should understand that, it should be you. You know what's at stake."

Kate got up and said through tears, "What makes you think they're going to listen to you this time? It's like a nightmare John, one I can't wake up from. I can't take it anymore. Let someone else lead the charge. There are lots of researchers who agree with you. Let's wait John, the time isn't right. We are in the middle of a republican administration and they will do anything to silence you. The energy lobby has too much power and influence."

Still pacing the floor, John said, "We can't wait any longer. There isn't any more time, it might be too late already. Kate, you've seen the data. If we don't make a drastic change in the release of CO2 in the next 5 years, the human race is doomed."

She said, "John, I understand what's at stake just as much as you do. But I'm afraid, John. These people will stop at nothing to shut you up and discredit your research."

Just then, the event coordinator peeked her head in the door and said, "Five minutes."

John said, "Look Kate, after the conference, we'll get away for a few weeks. I still need to collect air quality samples in the south pacific, we can make it a working vacation. It's not as bad as you think. They are just trying to scare us. After this conference, after we present all the facts, the UN will have to act. I know they move like molasses, but several member countries are already in danger of flooding. This presentation could make all the difference. I have to believe that what I'm doing is going to make a difference. If it's not me then who? Maybe we can get something started. Remember when we protested the war? No one paid any attention until thousands marched in the streets and cop cars were set on fire. Maybe

that's what it will take now, but it has to start somewhere."

He stopped pacing and as he reached out for Kate he said,

"I've got to go through with this Kate, there's just too much at stake."

She held him tight, and with tears in her eyes she said, "Oh John, I know you're doing what you think is right, but at what

cost? Then she kissed him and said, "Good luck."

John turned and looked at his research assistants and said as he walked towards the door leading to the stage, "It's showtime." As John walked out on the wings of the stage, he felt like the weight of the world was on his shoulders.

The Kennedy Center Jazz band was just finishing the quiet dinner music as the UN secretary for the global climate initiative, was making his way towards the dais. Thanking the assembled group and after telling a bad joke he said, "It is with great pleasure to introduce our featured speaker of the evening. With an alphabet soup of degrees, it is my honor to present, Dr. Jonathan Loveton."

"Good evening Ladies and Gentlemen, scientists, distinguished guests and members of the press. Let me start with a quote from Russian scientist Vernadsky, who as early as 1929 said: "Life appears as a great, permanent and continuous infringer on the chemical 'dead hardness' of our planet's surface ... Life therefore is not an external and accidental development on the terrestrial surface. Rather, it is intimately related to the constitution of the Earth's crust, forms part of its mechanism, and performs in this mechanism functions of paramount importance, without which it would not be able to exist.

Recently I have been called many things. A crazy, deranged lunatic and worse. And I can accept that. Because, throughout human history, great thinkers, scientists and innovators have been arrested, silenced, banished, and even burned at the stake, for challenging authority and the status quo. From Galileo to Einstein, scientists have faced criticism and sometimes even death. And as I stand here today, I myself have been subject to the same ridicule and threats. Yes, even in modern times, there are some among us that would silence the truth. Turn a blind eye to the facts staring them in the face and doom the human race to virtual extinction. Don't think it can't happen to us? Just remember the Romans, the Egyptians, the Mayans, and who can forget the mighty dinosaurs.

But do not lose all hope. Yes, you all know me by now, I have bad news. And I have some good news. But first let me get to the heart of the matter. And I can't emphasize this enough. The Earth is dying a slow death, and we can stop it, but we have to act now!

Let me outline some of the issues facing the future of the human race as we understand it in the modern era.

As he says this a curtain opened behind him and on a large screen is a picture of the earth taken from space.

Our solar system evolved, from remnants of a massive supernova, and from it, the earth slowly formed some 4.5 billion years ago. The Earth slowly evolved from stardust, to a molten ball floating in space. Over time a rocky crust formed around an iron core. And as the earth cooled, another billion years passed, and the earth was bombarded by comets and icy debris from the gravity of our sun and pulled towards earth. Oceans formed, and the miracle of life began. How, who knows? Was the earth seeded with life from one of these distant interlopers? We may never know.

Somehow life evolved in the oceans and as these simple microorganisms took in carbon dioxide, giving off life sustaining oxygen, the earth was transformed from a barren wasteland to a terrestrial garden. Throughout eons of time the earth was changed by life itself as it slowly evolved over billions of years. From microorganisms evolving in the earth's oceans creating oxygen, to the growth of land plants, swamps, forests, rainforests, prairies, mountains and deserts.

The earth itself acts like a giant self-sustaining organism. Each system dependent on one another, not unlike the organs in the human body. And like the human body, the earth is made up of thousands of ecosystems each dependent on one another for survival. You can look at the earth like a body. A celestial body. And right now, that body is sick. It's not dying yet, but without treatment, this celestial body that sustains life as we know it will die and we will die with it.

My friends and colleagues, as many of you know, due to the continuous burning of stored carbon in the form of fossil fuels, chemical, and industrial pollution, toxic oil spills, agricultural runoff, deforestation and ocean acidification. I could go on and on, but you get the picture.

The balance of nature that has created and sustained life on earth for 3.5 billion years has been irreparably harmed. And I need to clarify that human activity is not just the primary cause; it is the only cause!

At some point in the not too distant future, most of all the obtainable resources of earth will be depleted. I know for most of you that is hard to imagine. But modern humans have only been around for 150,000 years. And the first industrial revolution began only 150 years ago. And in that short amount of time, we have poisoned the oceans, nearly used up all obtainable oil, changed the atmosphere and the oceans, and started the 6th great extinction. The World Wildlife Foundation estimates that 6,000 species are going extinct every year. How long will it be until we are on that list?

Not convinced. At some point in time, in the not too distant future, all of the earth's resources will be used up. Oil and natural gas reserves will run dry. Rare earth minerals will be depleted, etc... etc... etc.

Let me start with one of the earth's most important and most overlooked eco-systems, the world's oceans.

The screen behind him changed to a large panoramic view of the ocean.

Three quarters of this planet is covered by ocean water. And I might add, marine vegetation is responsible for 70% of the earth's oxygen production. Let me repeat that, marine vegetation is responsible for 70% of the earth's oxygen production. So basically, without a healthy, functioning ocean, the human race as we know it will cease to exist. Humans have the largest brains by far of any animal on the planet, except for our distant cousins, dolphins and whales. Animals with large brains require high levels of oxygen in the atmosphere to survive. Let me read between the lines here for you. Without a healthy ocean, humans will die. Period, end of story.

The unabated release of stored carbon into the atmosphere will poison the oceans beyond repair. The long-term effects of this poisoning is defined as ocean acidification. As in any ecosystem, all ocean life is dependent on the delicate balance of the aquatic food chain. It starts with microorganisms which grow in and around coral reefs and then grows exponentially from there. The global acidification of the world's oceans will cause a catastrophic die off of coral reefs, setting in motion a chain reaction, affecting the entire global ecosystem.

As the coral reefs around the world die off, huge coastal dead zones will be created, choking off a vital component to the ocean's ecosystem, and endangering the ocean's oxygen regeneration system. Massive marine species die-offs will occur, resulting in catastrophic famine in coastal areas. And this is just the start of what's to come if we don't act now to save the earth and the human race from the 6th great extinction.

The screen now changed to a view of the earth from varying perspectives from small planes and helicopters.

But that's not the least of our worries. At some point the Earth will reach a tipping point. At what point that is, no one knows for sure. Some say not for 50 years, some say it's already too late. The fact is we may never know, until it is too late.

Now let me tell you, I first started working for NASA, in the 50s and 60s when we were all wide-eyed idealists. I actually began my climate research, studying conditions on other planets in our solar system.

That is what inevitably brought me to the study of earth's climate and ecosystems. So, I am a little embarrassed to say, I am giving away my age here, I have been studying climate change for over 20 years now.

When I first began my research as an undergrad at Stanford, I sounded the alarm and everyone, including many of my esteemed colleagues thought I was crazy. And yet, as we venture further and further towards the tipping point, we can see the drastic weather-related events that even small changes in global temperature can have around the world. In addition to weather related catastrophes, the melting of the arctic glaciers will set in motion an irreversible chain reaction.

The screen changed to the arctic covered in ice from space. And the image slowly changes to an arctic without ice.

As you can see in this first photo, the polar ice caps act as gigantic mirrors reflecting nearly 35% of the total sunlight reaching earth, (the image changes to present day, with a drastically reduced polar ice cap). As these vast ice sheets disappear, the result is a dramatic exponential increase in direct solar heat absorption at the poles, which will further increase the rate of the global mean average temperatures exponentially.

The screen changed to melting glaciers across the globe.

Due to greater heat absorption, glaciers will melt at rates never seen before. As this unprecedented melting continues, global sea levels are predicted to rise by as much as 10 feet in some areas, causing catastrophic flooding around the globe.

The screen changed to an artist's rendering of NY City, flooded like Venice.

Some think this will be an inconvenience to people living in coastal areas. Well I chose the site of this conference here in New York City, not only for the city's many amenities, but also to make a point. If as predicted, we have a sea level rise of 5 to 10 feet, this great city would be under water, just like Venice.

Imagine this city of 6 million people, a city where the first floor of every building from Queens to Manhattan, would be underwater and the streets become rivers, with water taxis and boats shipping goods here and there. And this fate will be repeated, in coastal communities all over the world.

If that's not bad enough. The increase in temperatures will turn the US Midwest farm belt into a desert. And due to a rise in winter temperatures, insects and diseases that used to die off during the cold winter months, will continue to thrive, devastating crops and causing pestilence and epidemics around the globe.

Now we have already seen an increase in the number and severity of major weather-related events and record setting fires in California and throughout the west. And that is just in this country alone in just the last few years. But the US is not an island. Even a small rise in ocean temperatures will increase the number and severity of hurricanes and typhoons, destroying already flooded coastal areas across the globe.

If we don't reverse course very soon. Vast regions once lush with vegetation, will be reduced to barren wastelands. Starvation and famine will ravage the poorest counties first. The UN food network's which sustain areas of Africa, will be canceled due to low food stocks in the host countries.

Africa will be the first continent, thrust into an all-out civil war for dwindling food supplies. NATO will be powerless to stop the bloodshed and warring tribes and nations will slaughter of millions of innocent civilians. Similar to the tragedy in Rwanda but on a continent-wide scale.

China, our friend to the east, the world's newest economic superpower, will declare martial law to prevent riots and looting. Thousands of Chinese will be killed by government backed troops during food riots. Again, similar to the Tiananmen Square massacre but on a much larger scale.

Here in America, as water, food and gasoline stocks are rationed, hundreds of thousands of angry citizens will protest new austerity measures. The National Guard and Army will be activated and sent into major cities to restore order. Travel restrictions will put in place to prevent further chaos.

All over the world, in every nation, and in every county, city and town; riots, looting, and mayhem will be rampant. Police, military and national guards will be helpless to stop the lawlessness. China and Russia will likely go to war over Russia's remaining natural gas supplies.

Under the guise of protecting America's vital interests, the U.S. will invade Saudi Arabia and other middle eastern countries. Moscow will threaten a preemptive nuclear strike against the US if our military cuts off oil supplies to Russian.

Ceasing on the uprising, foreign and domestic terrorists, will wreak havoc across the United States and around the world. Aside from the mass shooting and bombings, our most vulnerable targets are the oil and gas refineries and nuclear power and electric production facilities and substations around the world.

If you find what I'm telling you, hard to believe, I have in my possession, confidential reports from the department of defense, NASA the NSA, the CIA and government funded think tanks, that forecast these exact scenarios as inevitable, in the face of this growing threat.

Detailed in these reports, terrorists, foreign and domestic are likely to bomb bridges, and tunnels, hydro-electric dams, gas and coal fired power plants, refineries and nuclear power plants, causing the massive destruction across America and throughout the world.

The earth will be thrust into global turmoil. Crops devastated by drought, disease, and pestilence will be inadequate to feed the global population estimated to be 9.6 billion by 2050. Weather related disasters will increase exponentially putting even greater stress on already depleted resources.

Melting glaciers will cause ocean levels to rise 10 to 15 feet in some areas causing flooding of coastal regions on every continent. Famine will spread across the globe. Fresh water will become a scarce resource.

Over a period of 10 years, as estimated in these reports, riots and wars over precious resources will reduce the entire human population to between 200,000 to 400,000 survivors scattered across the globe, living as our ancestors did some 10,000 years ago.

If you don't believe me, I have a copy of a top-secret US government report outlining all of the things I have discussed here today. And to my friends at the NSA and the FBI, no I will not divulge my sources. Let's just say that there are some in government that see through the obfuscation of a government either to blind or dumb to see the forest through the trees.

But no matter, I have already distributed copies of these reports to all the major news organizations around the world prior to my speech today, along with a copy of my detailed climate change report.

So, what do have to look forward to 100 years after the 6th great extinction? Think that sounds bad, it gets worse. Humans will devolve over hundreds of years. The remaining humans will live in small tribes near the upper and lower regions of the continents. A 10,000-mile swath N and S of the equator will be virtually uninhabitable due to drought caused by extreme climate change. The remaining population will exist like humans did thousands of years ago. In a constant state of tribal warfare for limited resources.

I can sense your skepticism across the room because you

find what I'm saying hard to believe. Some of you refuse to believe in man-made climate change. For the rest, you, you find it hard to contemplate the end of modern civilization as we know it. But the facts are simple. These facts are hard to face. But the reality is, as the human population continues to grow unabated, we are a planet of vast but ultimately limited resources.

And as the global population continues to grow, and as new and emerging economies attain greater and greater wealth, the demand for our limited resources will eventually bring us to a combined crisis of limited supply and demand, and drastic climate change; the effects of which I have detailed in my lecture and in my report. This is as I see it, our future unless we act now!"

Just then, a loud explosion is heard outside the building and all at once the large ornate conference room is plunged into complete darkness. A small group of protesters break into the room and begin chanting, "We love coal, coal yesterday, coal today, coal tomorrow!" As the backup generators are activated, the emergency lights cast an eerie glow across the room. Dr. Loveton is whisked off stage by UN security and he and his wife Kate are escorted out a side exit, ushered into a waiting limo and returned to their hotel.

CHAPTER 2

John Loveton was born in New Zealand into a wealthy British family. His father, Robert, a noted biologist, passed on his love of scientific discovery to his only son John. His mother Bell, a brilliant scientist, studied at Cambridge and Oxford.

Young John Loveton, a child prodigy, graduated with a PhD from Oxford at 17 with a double major in advanced mathematics, theoretical physics and biology.

John went on to receive multiple degrees from MIT, USC and Stanford in math, chemistry, structural engineering and molecular biology. He married a beautiful research assistant with multiple degrees in electrical, and structural engineering and advanced degrees in the emerging fields of quantum physics and nanotechnology.

Together they held several patents, some secret, in the area of nanotechnology, robotics and chemical engineering. Their work was often for DARPA, a secret government agency, designing complicated systems for R&D in the fields of nuclear fusion, structural Nano technologies, robotics and advanced electrical engineering.

John began his interest in ecology, when on a family vacation, in the Brazilian rainforest; he witnessed the destruction of the environment in underdeveloped countries as they struggled to improve their standard of living. His father was studying the migration of the monarch butterfly and John was amazed by the immensity of the migration. Million and millions of monarchs traveled thousands of miles to this remote jungle to mate and escape the harsh winters of their northern habitats.

When his family returned the next year, he was horrified to find the forest being destroyed, cleared for lumber and farmland. He cried as he witnessed the dislocation of millions of breeding monarchs. He ran to his father, "papa, papa look, look they're destroying the forest. Oh papa, where will the butterflies go now?" As James, looked up at the rising moon in the pale light of an Amazon dusk, he said to his son, "I don't know maybe they'll fly up to the moon!"

"Oh papa, butterflies can't fly that high."

"Well, I'm sure they'll find a new home, the Amazon is a big place."

John returned to the Amazon in later years as a research assistant and he witnessed the unchecked deforestation of the Amazon rainforest and saw the monumental threat to the global ecosystem. Upon his return, he began studying the effects of deforestation on the global climate system. He realized the devastating effects of deforestation in remote areas and how it could impact the global bio-system.

While a grad-student and Stanford, he created the "Committee of Concerned Scientists" to research the effects of deforestation and industrialization around the world. Loveton brought in research assistants and scientists from many disciplines: atmospheric, oceanography, biodiversity, chemistry, etc.…

At first the team worked the project as sort of a hobby. Spending their spare time indulging the whims of a respected colleague. However, as each one began their explorations into their areas of expertise, they saw small changes in almost every system and subsystem they studied. In and of itself, each area of study was not significant however, taken as a whole they quickly realized the gravity of Loveton's prediction. Close examination of the data revealed subtle changes in almost every field of study. And the conclusions of the committee suggested an unmistakable trend.

Each event taken on its own was not seen as a reason for concern. But taken as a whole, they began to realize the dilemma we faced as a global community. Entire species and ecosystems were being threatened. And that even small changes in one group could have catastrophic effects on other seemingly unrelated systems.

The GAIA theory was born of this research. The theory postulated that; the earth is one giant ecosystem. In which, seemingly separate systems are dependent on the others for balance and equilibrium; that a symbiotic relationship exists between all living things. And that, modern human activities have thrown the cycle out of balance. His team concluded that the earth was unmistakably at a critical juncture. And if unabated, life on earth would begin to see drastic changes. More scientists were brought in and journal articles were written. The peer review process was begun and scientists from around the globe were pouring over the data.

As word among the scientific community spread, major players in energy, industry and politics took notice and began to intervene. A small but powerful group of energy industry insiders took notice. Calls to higher levels were made, funding was canceled, grants were pulled, and pressure was brought to bear against Loveton and his colleagues to end their investigation. One by one his loyal followers left, saying, "Look, without funding we can't work, so good luck I'm sure you'll find a way……"

Undeterred, Loveton vowed to press on. He continued his work with graduate assistants, funding the project with his own money. He said to anyone who would listen, "This work is too important to the future of mankind. I must continue my research!" He found a few kindhearted souls, mostly trust fund liberal types, and Hollywood celebrities who dedicate their huge fortunes to saving the dolphins, seals, orphans or whatever hot-button issue of the day got them the most notoriety. However, they were too interested in fundraising parties and tony celebrity dinners to really understand the implications of what Loveton was doing. It still was never enough. The breadth and depth of the research needed was beyond what he alone could do. Yet he doggedly pursued his mission, finalizing his report his exhaustive report.

CHAPTER 3

Dr Loveton created a theory on planetary evolution. The main premises of his hypothesis is that as our solar system evolved, from remnants of a massive supernova, the earth's evolution was changed by life itself as it slowly evolved over billions of years. From microorganisms evolving in the earth's oceans creating oxygen, to the growth of land plants, swamps, forests, rainforests, prairies and deserts etc. His theory suggested that the earth itself acts like a giant self-sustaining organism.

In other words, as life on earth evolved, the earth evolved with it, creating a symbiotic relationship between the earth and living eco–systems.

As man-made Co2 levels rise, the effects on global climate systems will began changing, altering the delicate balance. The delicate balance between life sustaining ecosystems and ecological calamity. Dr Loveton's observations and climate models predict the catastrophic consequences of global warming.

His climate models predict that if unabated, the earth will reach a tipping point, a point at which the earth's ecological balance, which has sustained life for 3.5 billion years, will be irreparably damaged. Loveton realized that even small changes in global temperature could have drastic effects around the world.

Once John had completed his climate science research, he embarked on a worldwide crusade to in his words," Save humanity from insanity." He lectured world leaders, scientists and leading industrialists, in many countries and in many forums, he pleaded his case to anyone who would listen. "We must stop this insanity now!" He declared again and again. "Carbon levels are reaching dangerous proportions. We must stop burning fossil fuels and transition to a renewable energy economy or we are certainly doomed."

His warnings went unheeded. He was ridiculed and lampooned in the national and international press around the world. He was nicknamed "Dr. Killjoy" and the "Doomsday Dr! "A raving lunatic", "He loves nature more than people," etc.... etc...

However, a small group of scientists and reporters begin looking at his findings and a paper is published in a small, obscure publication, giving some acknowledgement to his predictions.

As his message began to take hold, he started receiving threatening phone calls. His research grant was canceled, his position at the university was eliminated. Broken hearted and dejected, he decides to retreat to his boyhood home of Queenstown, New Zealand to contemplate the future.

He embraced the solitude of the farms and pristine countryside of his youth. On a clear spring morning, while walking through a pristine mountain prairie, he reached an overflowing spring. As he sat along the bank of the small pool, watching, as a group of ants gathering their eggs and moving to higher ground, saving their nest from the rising water.

He is struck by the awesome power of nature to adapt to a constantly changing environment. He looked up at the setting moon in the early dawn and formulated the beginning of an absurd idea. He muttered to himself, "*Why can't we just move to a new home too?*" It was at that moment; he had a vision. A vision to save the human race from certain extinction. In his mind's eye, he envisioned huge space colonies filled with the last remaining human beings in the universe.

His quest to save humanity began. Realizing that by the time people in power act to prevent the inevitable consequences of global warming, it would be too little too late.

John realized that he may never live to see his grand vision reach completion, however, he knew that without the visionary leadership of men like himself in the scientific community, the human race may not survive.

CHAPTER 4

Tom Loveton was only 10 years old when his father John Loveton was killed in a car crash. Young Tom grew up in the shadow of his father. Following in his father's footsteps he graduated from Stanford at 16 with advanced degrees in molecular biology and chemistry. Although Tom was aware of his father's accomplishments in science and engineering, he was unaware of his father's research on climate change and his mission to save humanity.

Seen as an unsavory chapter in his father's past, the family hid this area of his research from the young impressionable Tom. However, his father's estate allowed Tom the luxury of finding and exploring his true passion; teaching.

Tom found great satisfaction in teaching and invigorating young minds. Tom's gift as a teacher was quickly recognized and with his good looks and affable charm, he is given a prestigious position at one of the top college prep schools in the country. As a child prodigy himself he was given a position teaching classes in advanced placement chemistry and biology. But Tom saw a different future for himself and after 2 years, he moved to the inner city in NY to work with underprivileged kids in a broken-down slum. His kids were more street smart than book smart, but they were very tech savvy.

The kids in Tom's class struggled at first and protested about doing homework and studying things they didn't see as relevant in their life on the streets. But Tom was patient and persistent and prove to them that, given the right motivation, they could learn and succeed in a scholastic setting.

To interest and motivate his students, Tom used a unified subject teaching model. Using examples from everyday street life, he created an online virtual city. He used the model to teach pair real world events with school subjects. He compared econ, math, science, chemistry and sociology to actual events from their world. Econ: selling black market goods, and the laws of supply and demand.

Math: how to calculate estimated profits and losses. Science and chemistry: what are the chemical properties of the drugs used by people in their virtual city? How is the brain and body affected by the chemicals, good and bad? Sociology: what are the socio-economic factors that push and pull people into a life of drug dependency and crime? What are the social opportunity costs of drug use among and large population? Etc.....

Once he gained the respect of his students, he broadened their course work. As a class project, Tom began a study of the earth's ecosystems. As his young students progressed in their research, Tom was struck by what he saw at first as a statistical anomaly. "This can't be happening on this scale," he thought.

As a class they dove deeper into the research and Tom accidentally discovered a research paper written by his. Searching a database, he came across an obscure reference to a paper his father wrote in 1974 titled "The Gaia Hypothesis"

As his tech savvy students began posting their findings online and on social media sites. A secret group funded by the major oil companies that secretly torpedoed his father's work were watching. Unknown to him, all his life Tom had been secretly watched, his home and classrooms were bugged, his phones and computers hacked. When news of his student's discoveries was found, the group known only in secret circles, as the Knights Club. Sent in their fixers.

Yia, the quiet leader of the class, failed to show up on Monday. Thinking he stayed home to help his mom at the restaurant, Tom didn't give his absence a second thought. Yia, late for school as usual, saw a group of suspicious men approaching the broken-down building that served as a makeshift inner-city school. Yia confronted them and when he saw bulges of guns in their suit coats, he became suspicious. He took out his phone and tried taking their picture and they chased him through the city streets and back alleys. He easily lost his pursuers and doubled back.

At first, he thought he was the target of a band of thieves. However, the men chasing him were much too sophisticated in their dress and mannerisms to be ordinary criminals. His 1st inclination was that they were from the gang he ripped off back in Laos and was after him for revenge. But these weren't Laotians, and the Laotian gangs only used their own people for jobs like this. No, it had to be a mistake. Why would they be after him? It didn't make any sense. Since he brought his family to America he'd gone straight. He had to find out what they were after.

He contacted his cousin Duke and told him his plan. What Yia didn't know was that the men were professional mercenaries, former military black ops hired killers, and assassins. But Yia had some secrets of his own. And he knew the streets. Trained in the martial arts by his uncle Dai, a grand master, Yia could handle just about any situation. He'd could kill if necessary but would only do so in self-defense. He knew these men were serious and he didn't want to underestimate them. But first he had to find out more. He would let them find him, then lead them down into the tunnels were Duke and his crew would be waiting.

Realizing the rest of the class might be in danger, he led the team deep into the underground. He sent another one of his cousins, posing as a paperboy to deliver a message to Dr Loveton and the class. "Armed men were trying to enter the building. You are in danger, don't talk here, toss all cells, we are compromised, repeat, cells are compromised. Meet me at the red sail."

This a code name for the racing boat that Tom owned and kept on a city dock. Fearing for the safety of his class he said to the class, "Ok kids, time for a field trip." The class was used to Tom's idiosyncrasies, and childlike affinity for adventure.

In unison they shouted, "all right!" Not wanting to be seen leaving the building, Tom, had the kids leave their cellphones behind and clamor down the fire escape. Just as he was leaving, a call came through on his cell from his mother Kate. She was staying at her family estate on Nantucket Island. He picked up the call just as he was on his way out the window. She sounded winded and out of breath.

"Tom it's Nana, something terrible has happened. Tom, can you hear me?" Tom was distracted by the kids goofing around outside on the landing and didn't hear what she was saying. He put the call and speaker and set the phone on a table by the window.

As he slipped over the windowsill and on the fire escape, never hearing her desperate pleas, he yelled towards the phone, "Hey listen,

Mom, I can't talk right now, I'll get back to you later ok?" The kids were anxious to get going and all shouted "Where are we going," almost in unison.

"It's a surprise!" Tom said, trying to hide the fear in his voice. He led the way down the iron railing and onto the 2nd floor landing. He pulled the lever and released the latch holding the ladder, and it slid down to the street. One by one he guided the kids through the hole in the iron grate, down the ladder and onto the aged pavement.

Getting his bearings, he led the way through the alley and out onto the street. They ran a half a block up the crowded street and down into the subway station. Just as they left the school, the classroom door slammed open and two mysterious men, dressed in black stormed into the room. Seeing the open window, they looked out as the kids were climbing down the fire escape ladder. They stayed just long enough to rifle through Tom's files and then stormed out the door, down the hall and out onto the street, just in time to see Tom and the kids running into the subway.

Tom had recently had a feeling like he was being watched. He couldn't put a finger on it, but he was beginning to piece together recent events and memories from his past. He always wondered why his mother acted so strangely whenever he asked about his father. And then his recent discovery of his father›s secret work. And now Yia's disappearance. He had always had his suspicions about his father's death. Something just didn't feel right about the whole thing.

CHAPTER 5

Tom and his family were living in the foothills of Santa Monica on a former vinery. His father was a research professor at Stanford and traveled the world going from one scientific conference to another He'd been gone a lot, more than usual, and when he was home, he seemed distraught. He was distracted and detached, and he drank heavily. Tom would sometimes hear him arguing loudly on the phone with people late at night.

Tom's birthday was approaching; he was going to be 10. A big boy he thought. He father had always made it a priority, to be home for Tom's birthdays. But this year it seemed as if his dad hardly noticed him anymore. Then suddenly, three days before the big day, his dad rushed off to the airport, mumbling something about a conference he had forgotten about.

He returned, after midnight the day before his Tom's birthday. He rose before sunrise, and waking the sleeping boy he said, "Now Tom, I know today's your birthday, but daddy has to leave, um, and go away for a while…. I don't know when I'll be back … but you promise daddy you'll be a good boy." And he hugged little Tom like he never wanted to let go. He left Tom's room and was gone. Tom never saw him again.

Tom's birthday came and went without even a call from his dad. Tom did his best to enjoy himself at the birthday party his mother planned. But in the back of his mind his thoughts were of his dad, and his abrupt departure. He half expected him to burst through the door at any minute, with an arm full of presents and a big bear hug. But as his mother was cleaning up from the party, and he was saying goodbye to the last of his friends, his dad was still a no show. His mother made the best of it by saying, "Well you know how busy your father's been lately, always running off at the last minute from one conference or lecture to another. I'm sure he'll call before bedtime".

As Tom was getting ready for bed, the phone rang. He was brushing his teeth; his mom answered the phone, expecting a call from her husband. It was the Marin county sheriff's office. They had a beach house just north of Malibu and she knew sometimes John would go there when he needed to be alone. Apparently, they had found John's car at the bottom of a cliff. It appeared that he was driving too fast after a brief rain and skidded off the pacific coast highway. She always told him he drove too fast. The car was a wreck. But they couldn't find John. No sign of him. After a thorough Coast Guard search of the coastline they found not a trace.

It was as if he had vanished into thin air. "Ma'am I can't explain it. There isn't even any blood at the scene. We'll keep looking of course but, with high tide and all, it doesn't look good. I'm very sorry."

Tom, listening from the doorway and assumed it was his daddy, 'Mommy, mommy I wanna talk, where is he, where's daddy?" She tried to hide her emotions, but Tom could always tell when his mother was upset.

She said through a veil of tears, "No dear, it's not your father, just one of his clients again. Go on…. go up and get ready for bed dear…mommy will be right in."

The boy sensed the tension in his mother's voice and said, "Mommy, is everything, alright? Where's daddy?"

She burst into tears from behind the half open door. "Just get ready for bed honey, mommy will read you a story." He could hear sobs between her words. But being a good boy, he finished getting ready for bed and was playing with some of his new toys as his mother came in, just then the phone rang. The private line in his father's study.

"Just a minute dear," his mother said as she went to answer the phone. The study was downstairs and was right below Tom's room. He could often hear is father's' late-night conversations, so when his mother went to answer the phone, he lay quietly, hoping to hear something. "Oh, dear god, are you alright?" she said a little too loud. She continued talking in a whisper, and when she returned to tuck little Tom into bed, she seemed different somehow.

CHAPTER 6

Tom had a feeling that his life was somehow starting to spin out of control. Gathering the kids together, they headed through the back alleys for the 7th street subway, which would take them to the harbor. His thoughts turned to Yia. What was this all about? He knew about Yia's past.

Yia was born on the streets of Laos. His parents were sold into slavery by a local gang and worked the underground textile mills in Vietnam. When Yia was old enough, he escaped and joined a gang, the only way for a young boy to survive alone on the streets. Yia was smart, smarter than most. He taught himself to read and learned math by running a numbers racket out of Chinatown.

Soon he was head of the Wai Ching gang. A step up from the band of thieves he used to run with. By running numbers and selling, guns and drugs on the street, he was able to buy his parents freedom. He finished with one final job, then took his parents to NYC. He was only 14 when they arrived. Once he did, his mother made him swear that he would go back to school. Get a college degree, and become a Dr., her lifelong dream for him.

A warning from Yia had to be taken seriously. But what could it mean? He always had suspicions about his father's death, and since he had uncovered his hidden research, it all made sense now. He was certain his father's death was no accident. His inquiries into his death lead to nothing but loose ends. No body found at the scene; the cause of death was a presumed drowning. Whatever this was, he was certain it had something to do with his father's research on climate change and his untimely death.

Then he remembered his mother's' behavior. She became very distant, always distracted somehow, with a faraway look in her eyes. This was in the very early days of the internet. When only researchers were wired in, on very simple, overly large computers. His dad had one of the early, desktop models. A commodore 64, with a modem and a 14k connection, and he shared his research models with scientists from around the world. His mother, who, at the time had no interest in computers, and thought them to be a silly waste of time. But then after his father's death, she would sometimes spend hours in the study on his dad's old machine, with charts and graphs surrounding the desk.

"What are you doing mom," he'd ask, wanting her attention.

"Oh, nothing dear, I'll be right there." She'd always say.

She'd always come out of the office a little flustered. But why? He always thought. What was she doing in there? Late nights, always late at night.

They made their way to the subway and took the 7th street train to the Redline and down to Brooklyn. From there they walked to the Paerdegat Avenue Yacht and Racquet Club where Tom kept his 30-foot Bay Runner. As they entered the dock, he practically ran with the kids over to the boat. They jumped on board, and while he prepared the engines for a quick exit, Yia appeared out of the hatchway, and with a cautious look in his eyes, he said, "Yo teach, I hope this is ok? I didn't know where else to go."

Tom revved the engines as they cast off. Tom roared out of the marina, just as a black SUV pulled onto the docks. Four men in black suits ran out onto the pier, weapons drawn, cell phones in hand.

"What the hell is going on?" Tom thought as he navigated the narrow channel. He had no plans at this point as to where to go or what to do next. He was scared. Scared of exactly what he didn't know. But was he scared enough?

CHAPTER 7

As Tom pulled away from the dock, Yia appeared from the berth below. "What the hell was that all about" Tom yelled over the engines.

Yia warily raised his head and said, "I don't know, teach. I was on my way to class and these scary looking dudes were about to enter the school and then when I tried to take their picture they chased after me. I lost them in the underground, and doubled back, and made my way here. These guys are scary teach. They're wearing bullet proof vests and carrying Glocks."

Looking warily at his student Tom said. "Well I'm glad you're ok. When I got your message, I was worried. Did you find out anything about what they want?"

Yia explained, "I don't know, after I ditched them, I doubled back and heard them saying something about plan B."

Regaining his macho exterior Yia said, "Yo teach, what are we gonna do now?"

Tom was busy navigating the channel out of the harbor and concerned for his kids. He knew this was a serious situation and required some quick thinking. Tom decided to take the kids up the coast to Nana's place.

Nana's, as it was called, was the family's vacation home on Nantucket Island. It had originally belonged to his great grandmother on his mother's side. It was now the family summer home but Tom's mother Kate, spent more and more time there every year. Preferring the cool summer days on the cape to the dreary heat of their north county estate in N.Y. He thought about her call back in the classroom, but having ditched their cellphones, he had no way to call her back.

He made his way up the coast and tried the ship to shore radio. He knew it was unlikely anyone would be at the boathouse, but it was worth a try. He got no response and checking his satellite navigation system set a course for the island.

There was a dock and a boat house in the quiet cove, and a guest house next to the stately main house. Kate currently had full time caretakers that lived on the property year-round. A retired military couple that Tom's dad used to know kept up the property, a 20-acre estate, on a hill overlooking the Atlantic coast.

The sky was clear as they motored up the coast, and Tom was feeling a little better now that he had a plan. Yia had said to ditch their phones. Now he was glad he did. If these guys were as sophisticated as Yia said, they could probably track their cell GPS coordinates. He flicked on his satellite navigation system to see what other ships were in the vicinity. He saw a couple of day sailors a few freighters and a sport boat, but that was about it. He thought he was getting a little paranoid. But after what just happened, he thought better safe than sorry. He tried the ship to shore radio again but got no response.

He pulled up close to the bay, watchful of anything unusual. He circled the inlet a few times and slowly entered, killing the engine and coasting up to the dock. He got out his pole and pushed the boat up into the slip. With the help of the kids he tied up to the dock and stepped on the floating pier.

Trying to sound optimistic he helped the kids out of the boat and up to the boat house and said, "Hey kids, stay here in the boat house while I check things out before we go up to the house."

Tom warily walked up the 50 or so, well-worn stone steps to the yard, keeping a watchful eye for any movement. It was another 50 yards to the house, and he was a little out of breath when he reached wooden steps attached to the back porch. He was puzzled that the dogs weren't around. After his father died, Kate had taken a liking to large police dogs. She said she was lonely, and they were good company, but he always suspected something more. They were always just a little too well trained for normal house pets.

But there was nothing, not so much as a bark. He thought, *"Maybe she went into town."* He found the back-porch door unlocked, which wasn't unusual this time of year. Nobody locked their doors on Nantucket Island, but still something bothered him. The dogs, or lack of dogs? He wasn't sure. But something had his radar up. He searched the sizable downstairs and found nothing amiss. Except for the living room phone, which was off its cradle, lying on the floor. And the pillows were in slight disarray. Kate always insisted on such a neat and orderly house.

He called out, "Nana, Nana ...is anyone home?" No answer. Now surely, if the dogs were around, they would have barked, hearing his voice. But nothing, no Nana and no dogs....

He took a quick look in the kitchen to see if anything there was to eat. He found a full fridge, and thought, "*Well it looks like Nana's expecting company.*" She had a large family and was always entertaining.

As he grabbed a soda from the fridge he thought, "*Maybe she took the dogs to visit one of the neighbors?*" He started to relax, and decided the coast was clear. As he carefully made his way down the rickety wooden steps he wondered, "*Was it safe to stay here?*" It wouldn't be hard to trace him to the family retreat. But he still couldn't understand what anyone would want with him and the kids?

After Tom left the kids and went up to the house, they decided to explore the old 3 story wood and stone boat house. The first floor was built with a rusty boat ramp and had a large winch for hauling boats up the ramp for off-season storage. There were several antique sailboats and a couple of wooden Chris Craft motorboats on movable boat dollies spread out on the dusty cement floor. Not finding anything of interest there, they trampled up the tall stairs, and as they reached the top, they burst into the large observation deck overlooking the quiet bay and breakwater, protecting the property from the reach of the cold harsh Atlantic.

The third-floor observation deck was actually a maritime museum of sorts. The large room was full of old furniture, taken from old whaling ships that sailed these waters before the days of steamers. Antique sailing equipment, old nautical charts and original oil paintings depicting every style of craft that sailed the ocean waters since before the days of Columbus, adorned the knotty pine walls of the 200-year-old former yacht club house.

Julie's attention was drawn to an antique table sized radio, and as she tried to tune in her favorite radio station, she was oblivious to the fact that the 70-year-old devise wasn't even plugged in and hadn't carried a tune for more and 30 years.

Tim and Allison were looking through the cupboards near an old cook stove for something to eat. They didn't hear the jet boat quietly approach the bay, cutting its engines, and poling up to the dock, the same way Tom had done earlier.

The men in the boat, were quiet and cautious. They pulled their boat alongside Tom's, shielding it from view of the boat house. Then they quietly slipped onto the dock. Working with military precision, one of them checked Tom's boat, and quickly cut the fuel lines.

They could hear the kids laughing and horsing around up on top floor. One of the men took a small pair of binoculars from a pouch around his belt and scanned the house for any sign of Tom. He just made out Tom's silhouette as he crossed the patio onto the porch. He made a hand gesture to one of his comrades and they hurried up the steps to the boat house.

Yia was desperately trying to get the old phone on the bar to work, but after years of sitting in the salty air of the north Atlantic the old rotary phone was nothing more than a decoration. His smart phone was out of juice and he had no way of recharging it. He had just given up on the phone when the 3 mysterious men burst into the room. Yia, taken by surprise, realized that any attempt to fight 3 armed men would only endanger his friends, so he let himself be captured without too much of a struggle. He wasn't prepared for the syringe as it plunged into his thigh. He lost consciousness instantly.

The men entered the room, first tazing then drugging the unsuspecting kids as they were quickly captured. They then carried the kids one by one down to the boat and quietly eased back into the bay. One of the men polled the boat along till they were out of the inlet. Only starting the quieted engines once they left the confines of the cove.

As Tom went down to the pier, he expected to see the kids running around getting into trouble, but there was nothing but silence. He shouted down towards the water, "Hey kids let's go inside, the coast is clear." He was just kidding, sort of. But there was no sign of them. He checked the boathouse, thinking they were hiding on him for a joke. But when he looked out the window, he saw a large boat just leaving the bay. Odd he thought, they had a private inlet with the only dock, then he saw Hattie's blond hair, blowing the breeze as she was hauled through the hatchway into the cabin of the black boat. His mind screamed, *"It's them, they somehow followed us. Dam! How could I be so stupid?"* He ran down to his boat but saw the gas line had been cut. Whoever had taken the kids knew how to disable a boat, quickly and quietly. Yes, these guys were pros. But want did the hell did they really want?"

Realizing the kids had been abducted, Tom ran back to the house. He picked up the phone on the porch, only to find no dial tone. *"Shit,"* he thought, *"I should have known."* he said to himself, as he ran out into the living room to check the phone there. Again, no dial tone. From there he went to the den where his dad had his office. He pushed open the partially open door looking for another phone. The den had been ransacked, with drawers pulled open and left on the floor. Pictures tore off the walls and bookshelves upended, even the carpet had been pulled up, as if someone was looking for a secret safe or something.

Tom then ran to the caretaker cottage hoping to find a working phone there. It wasn't uncommon for the Island to have occasional outages, but with the kids taken and Nana and the dogs gone, he was worried.

When he opened the door to the small cottage, he called out, "Dale?.........Buffy?" He couldn't believe his eyes, there was blood everywhere. The two dogs were lying in a pool of blood on the living room floor. As the afternoon sunlight cast shadows through the shuttered windows, he saw Dale and Buffy on the kitchen floor, there ashen bodies askew. He knelt down holding Buffy's hand, it was covered in blood.

He could almost taste the metallic tinge of blood in the back of his throat as he retched, gagging to stop from spilling his guts all over the bloody room. His thoughts immediately went to his mom. Acutely aware of imminent danger, his thoughts went to Kate and her recent call, he was desperately worried about her and wondered where could she be?

As these thoughts raced through his mind, he heard sirens in the distance. At first, he desperately wanted to call the police, but now he wasn't so sure. He was the only one here, and now he was covered in blood. With his stranded at the boat at the dock, how could he explain this…he needed time to think, the sirens were getting closer, they'd be here any minute.

With his heart racing, he decided the only thing he could do was stay and try to explain. Explain what? That he and his class were being chased through the city by mysterious men in black suits, and that they came here to get away, only to find Nana gone, the kids kidnapped, and the dogs and Dale and Buffy dead. It was too much for even him to believe. No, his only option was to run. Run and buy some time to figure things out. But where and how?

"Of course, the ultralight!" He said to himself. Nana had bought one a couple of years ago, part of her bucket list she claimed. She only flew it a couple of times a year but insisted that Dale keep it flight ready all summer, just in case; she always said. In case of what he'd always thought. Now the crazy contraption might just save his neck.

He'd flown it once, several years ago when she first got it. As a grad student and research assistant, he frequently flew into far off regions of South America, remote areas without proper airports, and still held a pilot's license.

As quickly as he could, he ran down to the shed where the small plane was housed. It was well across the yard, opposite the driveway and he ran through the clearing and entered the wooded path just as the police cars pulled into Nana's driveway. He knew it wouldn't be long before the bodies were discovered, and he had to be quick. He needed to be in the air before they realized he was here and gone.

Separated by a thicket made up of old willows and tangled vines, the ultralight was kept in a small makeshift hanger, in a field adjacent to the house. He ran down the dirt path, sweat dripping off his mess of hair. He got to the hanger only to find the large shed doors ajar and plane gone! Nana must have escaped in the small plane. But where could she have gone? He couldn't wait around wondering, he had to get away and fast.

He could hear more sirens in the distance, and felt the hairs on his neck rise, *"What the hell I'm I going to do now?"* He thought as he quickly assessed his options. It was then he remembered the Johnson's private marina. Yes. It was fenced in, but if the old tree fort was still there maybe he could sneak in undetected and somehow borrow a boat.

The old tree house was built by Tom's great uncle and overlooked the Johnson property. Tom ran down the overgrown path until he reached base of an old maple tree at least 5 feet thick. He slowly made his way up the broken steps of the old ladder and as he reached the top, he glanced back towards the house and saw a group of Sheriff Deputies scouring the property. He knew he had to act fast, but he hadn't been to the Johnson's place since he was a kid.

Memories of his first crush briefly entered his mind. Polly was two years older than him and they used to play "house" together in the Johnson's old hunting shack when they were kids. She was cute in a Tom boy sort of way, tall with reddish blond hair and freckles. He hadn't seen her in years despite their similar interests in ecology. He prayed now that she'd be there. She was now the only person on the Island that he could trust.

He scrambled up the rest of the ladder to the tree house door, or what was left of it. The old "fort" as he and his cousins used to call it, was nearly collapsing around the trunks of the old tree that held it so tightly. He carefully crept along the rotting wood floor, staying low to avoid detection and opened the trap door which opened on the Johnson side of the floor. There used to be an old rope ladder that they would drop down during one of their imaginary adventures, but it was nowhere to be found.

He looked around for anything he could use, it was a 30-foot drop and he couldn't risk jumping from that height. He was just about to give up when he saw an old rope coiled up in a dark corner of what was left of the floor. He quickly tied one end of the rope to a sturdy tree limb and let the rest fall. It didn't reach all the way to the ground, but it was close enough. He just hoped the rope would hold his weight as he lowered himself down, and ten feet from the ground the old rope broke, and he fell onto the hard-knotted roots surrounding the old tree.

As he stood and gingerly and rubbed his now sprained ankle, he tried to remember the layout of the huge estate. The Johnson property was home to 6 large New England style mansions, one for each of the original family members. If memory serves him right, the Johnson boat house held one of the finest collections of antique boats on the east coast. If only he could find one fueled and ready.

Nursing his sore ankle, he hopped as fast as he could through the thicket and bramble. The 100 yards or so to the main boat house seemed to take forever as the pain in his now swollen ankle got worse with each step. As he reached the grass surrounding the old log cabin styled warehouse, he slowly made his way around the back side, pushing back waist high weeds as he went.

He had to climb down a pile of small boulders to reach the shoreline and holding tightly to an old tree limb, he peered around the corner to see a modern racing yacht, tied up to the dock.

He waited a few seconds and with no one in sight, climbed up the wooden supports of the old pier and stepped on to the old dock for the first time in almost 10 years. He praised his luck as he looked into the beautiful craft and saw his old sweetheart from what now seemed like a lifetime ago. Polly was busy working on a canvas cover, and as she turned to grab a tool, almost jumped for joy when she saw Tom. "Oh my god Tom! What are you doing here? What's it been what 10 years?" she said as she reached out to hug him.

He almost fell as he limped over the railing, and reaching out to her, he said, "Poll, I'm so glad to see you, I'm in real trouble, it's Dale and Buffy. God I can't believe it Polly, but they're dead! Murdered! The dogs too. It's terrible. I need your help."

Choking back tears, he said, "I found them in the guest house, and Nana's gone in the ultralight. I have no idea what's going on, but my kids, my students were taken, kidnapped by men in a speedboat. Listen, I know it sounds crazy, but someone is after us. They chased us through the city, and we made it to the harbor and escaped in my boat. I don't know what's going on, but I need your help. You're the only one in the Island I can trust." And looking over at the beautiful racing yacht he said, "How soon can we leave."

Polly, still trying to process everything Tom was saying just looked at her old friend and said, "Tom, listen to me, we should go up to the house and call the police, I'm sure they can figure out what's going on, come on, my dad's having tea out on the back porch. He'll know what to do."

"No! Polly, listen to me! We can't go to the police, not until I can figure this out. It's got something to do with my dad. I'm sure of it. Something about his research, and his disappearance. Polly, they even killed the dogs! I was at school when I got a message from one of my students. He said we were in danger and to meet him at the harbor. We went out the fire escape and they chased us through the city. We barely made it off the dock before they caught us. They had bullet proof vests and were armed. I don't know what they want, but it's real and it's serious. Is the boat ready to go?"

"Yes, but Tom, I beg you, let's talk to my dad first."

"No, Polly, I can't explain now. The Sheriffs are going to looking for me, Polly. I tried to call the police when I found Dale and Buffy, but the phones were out, and before I could even blink, I heard sirens. Polly, someone is trying to set me up. I can't just wait here to be arrested. I brought my students here to get away from the men chasing us in the city, but someone got here before we did and killed Dale and Buffy. Then they took the kids from the boat house. Nana somehow got away. The first thing I have to do is find the kids, please Polly. You're the only person I can trust. Will you help me?"

"Tom, I've known you my whole life, I mean you were the first boy I ever kissed. Yes, I'd do anything for you, but we can't just leave, not without contacting my dad. I've got a sat phone in the boat. Let me at least call up to the house and let my him know what's going on?"

"Polly, they could be here any minute. God damn it! Look at my clothes, I've got blood all over me. I can't just wait here for them to arrest me. Cause that's what they're going to do. I have to find my kids, Polly, you are my only hope."

"Ok, ok, I'll take you anywhere you want to go, but I can't just leave without telling my dad, he'll be worried. I'm taking care of him after his stroke."

"Alright, but we need to leave right now! Can we call him after we put out to sea? My boat is still at the dock. It won't take them too long to figure out where I am. Where else could I go?" And as Tom stepped on to the fore deck, Polly realized that he was injured.

"I'm sorry Tom I didn't realize you were hurt, let me help you." And as she reached out for Tom's hand, they could hear the baying of hounds approaching the property. The high fence would keep them out for a while, but Polly knew they'd just break the lock on the fence gate up by the access road.

"Ok Tom, just prime and start the engines, and I'll cast off. Even if they try to follow us, this is the fastest boat on the coast.

We'll be halfway to New York before they even know we're gone. Let's get going."

Polly carefully guided Tom to the cockpit and pointed him towards to primer and ignitions switches. She said, "Hold the primer switch down for 30 seconds, when this light turns green, start the engines by pressing these two buttons. Then rev the engines with this lever here, and by then I'll be ready to cast off."

By the baying of the hounds Tom knew that they didn't have much time. The sleek tri-hull racing boat was actually built by the Johnson outboard motor corporation, for which Polly was the VP of the pro racing division.

As Tom primed the engines, Polly pulled in the mooring lines and secured the dock bumpers to the customized hull. They could hear sirens in the distance and Tom expected to see the Sheriff's hounds running up the dock at any second.

Anxiously waiting for the green light, Tom couldn't get the image of Dale, Buffy and the dogs out of his mind. *Why on earth would anyone kill two innocent people?* Tears were streaming down his face as he heard a beep, and through his watery eyes he saw the green light flash off and on. He knew this wasn't the time for grieving, he had to stay focused. Finding the kids now was his top priority.

With the dock bumpers firmly secured to the custom racks, Polly threw Tom a custom racing vest and pushed into the adjacent seat and said, "Let's get underway, they'll be here any second. Get the vest on and strap yourself in."

Each of the four top side seats in the custom racing boat were equipped with a three-point racing harness. Tom was just struggling to attach his seat belt as Polly revved the engines. Tom could hear dogs barking and people yelling above the roar of the huge turbocharged diesels, and as they rocketed out of the small harbor, he looked back to see five Sheriff Deputies running up the pier.

Up at the house, Bill Johnson was just waking up from a nap on the porch when he heard dogs barking and saw a group of Sheriff Deputies, running down to the boat house. He heard the racing boat roar out of the harbor, and walked out onto the lawn as Sheriff Wilson, returning from the boat house approached the porch.

"Hey Ken," he said as he approached the big man.

Ken Wilson had been Sheriff on the Island for more than 20 years and knew all of the residents like old friends.

A worried look on Ken's face troubled the old man. "What's going on Ken?" he said as he looked out to sea.

"Hey there Bill, well we're actually looking for Tom. Tom Loveton, you know, Kate's boy, you haven't seen him around, where have you? We thought we saw him in Polly's boat as she left the bay."

Bill could sense the urgency in Ken's voice and said, "Nah, you know Ken I haven't seen that boy since I caught him making moves on Polly 20 years ago."

"Well Bill, there's been um, well, I'm not sure how to say this Bill, but Dale and Buffy are dead. It's pretty bad. Looks like they were murdered. We're not sure just yet what happened but Tom's boat is down at the dock and he seems to have vanished into thin air. We just want to talk to him you know, make sure he's ok. And by the way, Kate is missing. Not sure if she left the Island but we're looking for her too. We've got all our men on it Bill, there's no reason to be worried. But we have a bit of a mess here. Nothing like this has happened on this Island in recent memory.

With a concerned look, Bill said, "Well Ken, I'll let you know if I see Tom or Kate. Polly's on call with the Marine rescue squad and she's always running off saving one animal after another. I'll have her give you a call when she gets back. Until then, unless you have a warrant, I'm going to have to ask you to leave my property."

A little surprised by Bill's' request, Ken said, "Well Bill, this is a murder investigation after all, and well, we want to be sure all our residents are safe."

Now with some irritation in his voice, Bill said, "I think we're safe here, so if you don't mind, I don't like having an army of Deputies camping out on my back lawn."

"Yes of course Mr. Johnson, we'll be on our way, just have Miss Polly give us a call down to the station after she's done saving the planet."

Bill watched as the Deputies made their way back to the Loveton Property. He had just made it up to the porch, when the phone rang. It was Polly.

After clearing the bay, as Polly gave Tom a custom racing helmet she said, "There's a com link built into each one, so we can talk. But first I need to call my dad." She got out her waterproof sat phone and connected through the island landline network.

"Yeah hey dad, um ah listen, I got a distress call, yeah there's a beached whale, on the north coast. What? The police? No, I haven't seen Tom. They said what, that I helped him escape? Escape what?"

Her father shared his conversation the Sheriff and said that he sent him on his way, but that she should give him a call as soon as she returned.

The summer sun was still on the horizon and although there was another 3 hours of sunlight, a small squall was brewing to the east darkening the skies and was descending on the Island. With a full set of tanks, Polly knew that they had three to four hours of fuel depending on their speed and weather. She could easily outrun the small storm but had no idea where to go. At 70 knots, it only took a few minutes for the world class racing boat to make it 3 miles out to sea.

She pulled back on the twin racing throttles and said into the microphone built into her helmet, "Tom what the hell is going on?"

Still in shock from being chased by bloodhounds and the Island security forces, Tom was speechless. "Listen Tom, we've got to make a plan, I know you've obviously been through a lot today but what are we going to do now?"

Tom spoke into his helmet and Polly reached over and adjusted the built-in com-link and he said, "Listen Polly, I can't thank you enough for getting me out of there, I had no idea you had anything like this in your collection."

"It's a prototype, one of dad's hobbies. I'm glad to help, but we need a plan here."

"Yes, of course, um, I think we should make our way back down the coast, in this we should be able to catch up with whoever took the kids before they make for their harbor. I saw the boat as it left the bay, it was about a 50-footer, all black, a Sea Ray."

"I can do better than that," she said as she activated the state-of-the-art satellite navigation system. "This will show every craft within a thousand miles. Now what kind of boat was it?"

Looking at the impressive display, Tom said, "It was like mine, a Sea Ray, but bigger, probably a 50-footer. All black."

"All right, that shouldn't be too hard to find, providing we can see them before they make it into whichever harbor there going for. Let's see, I'll narrow the search area, and hopefully I can spot them. Here, that looks like them. There it is, what do you think? It looks like there making for Jones Bay. I think we can catch up with them before they make the dock, but strap in, if we're going to catch them, we're going in at near full speed."

Tom put his helmet back on and reattached his racing harness, and as promised, Polly pushed down on the throttles and the 60-foot racing yacht took off like marlin after prey.

Although, they had about a 15-minute head start, the kidnapper's small day runner was no match for the world class racing boat. The squall had kicked up some offshore wind and the seas were up to 5 to 7 feet and choppy.

With the help of a set of waterproof binoculars, Tom located the boat just as they were entering the breakwater. "There they are," Tom said, as he handed the sport glasses to Polly. "We've got to sneak up on them."

"I don't know how sneaky we can be in this thing, but we can keep an eye on them," Polly said as she slowed the craft down to around 20 knots.

Fortunately, their prey was heading towards a busy public harbor, where their boat wouldn't raise too many suspicions. Polly often fueled many of the family's fleet here, and she was friends with the harbormaster and her crew.

Polly got up on her knees to see over the massive cowling of the racing boat. "There they are," she said as she steered past the break-water, "They're heading for the short-term docking area. We should be able to follow them right up to the dock, as long as you keep your helmet on, they won't suspect a thing."

Polly expertly steered her boat to a berth in view of the other boat. She was used to the stares as people from all over the harbor descended on their pier like moths to a flame.

Polly said into her mic, "Tom there's a team racing jacket on the bench down below, put that on over your life vest and with your helmet on, they'll never recognizer you. Just pretend you're one of the crew."

"Good idea," he said as he gingerly dashed below. Through all the commotion, he'd forgotten all about his sprained ankle and he tripped banging his head on the door frame. He found the team racing jacket just where Polly said it would be and quickly made the change, putting the helmet on last as he made his way top side.

Polly was busy securing the boat and several dock hands were eagerly assisting the lovely boat captain, as several onlookers were gawking and taking pictures.

Tom wearily looked over the cockpit windshield as he tried to get a glimpse of the black Sea Ray tied up three berths over. He saw no sign of the kids, and the men had changed from their black suits into summer yachting attire. Very professional he thought, as he stepped as lightly as he could up onto the brightly colored deck.

Polly was back in the captain's chair as she talked loudly over the ship to shore radio. She had remover her helmet and let her long reddish blond hair blow in the light afternoon breeze. Thinking ahead, Polly had attached a personal com link to her racing jacket, so she and Tom could talk without him taking off his helmet.

She said that her friends at the harbor said the suspect's boat was docking for the night and just then a large 100-footer made for the next berth and pulled alongside the Sea Ray. In no time, several large men, all dressed in black, appeared out of nowhere and jumped off the super yacht, securing her to the dock. And just as quickly, they disappeared into the aft cabin behind darkly tinted windows.

"Well, it looks like our friends have some company," Polly said as she took Tom below.

"Ok what the hell do we do now?" Tom said as he removed his helmet. "We still have to rescue the kids."

As she changed into her black neoprene dry suit, Polly said, "Well I might have a plan. But it depends on what they do next. My guess is that they are going to wait until dark to move the kids to the larger boat. They were probably going to move them at sea, but with the weather the way it is, that would be too risky. We just got lucky they stopped here."

As she handed Tom another dry suit she said, "Now we really don't know what we are up against here. Are you sure you don't want to call the police?"

"What's this for?" Tom said as he stripped down and started pulling the thermal dry suit up his muscular legs.

As she helped Tom with his dry suit she said, "We have to blend in without being noticed. My day job is as a marine wildlife researcher. This is where NOAA stores the boats I use for my research. I tag seals and study their migrations."

Tom said desperately, "Well that's all fine and good, but how is that going to help us rescue the kids."

"Here, let me show you," Polly said as she opened a large waterproof canvas bag. "These for starters," she said as she pulled out a plastic case and removed several large tranquilizer darts. "I use these when I'm tagging sea lions. Each one has enough tranquilizer to put a 1000-pound male sea lion to sleep for over an hour."

As she loaded a pressurized air rifle with a cartridge holding 6 darts, she said, "We just have to wait till they make their move. These are accurate at up to 50 ft. If we're lucky, very lucky, we can rescue the kids without anyone getting seriously hurt. First we need to find out how many we are up against."

Tom was startled by Polly's immediate command of the situation but had his reservations about their chances of success. He turned Polly around and holding her by the shoulders looked into her beautiful green eyes and said, "Polly, wait a minute, you can't seriously expect the two of us to take on several armed men with just these darts. Where did you ever get the gumption to plan anything like this in the first place? When I knew you, you wouldn't even go near a daddy long leg spider."

Tossing her hair back and pulling it into a ponytail she returned Tom's stare and said, "Don't be silly Tom, I was in the navy for 4 years. That's how I funded my college tuition. "We just have to create a diversion. I figure there can't be more than 3 on the smaller boat and maybe 5 on the larger boat. We take out the men in the smaller boat first. If we're lucky, the men on the other boat will have some trouble with the local coast guard. And we can just ride off into the sunset. Stunned by the change in his old friend Tom said, "Polly, what are some kind of female Rambo?"

"Something like that," she said as she strapped on a scuba belt. She handed one to Tom and said, "Look, Tom, you're just going to have to trust me, I was a navy tactical ops specialist for 2 years. First of all, we have the advantage, we have the element of surprise, they certainly are not suspecting a direct attack. Second the marina is well lit even at night, so they don't dare bring any firearms out in the open. Third, the dart guns are completely silent, and I'm an expert marksman. It should be like shooting fish in a barrel. All I need you to do is create a distraction. As Polly prepped the dart guns, darkness descended on the marina.

Inside the larger boat, the team leader was assessing the situation. They hadn't counted on Tom's escape from the Island. He was supposed to be in custody for the murder of the Jones and the drowning of his students, forcing him into custody where he would be blackmailed into cooperating. But without Tom in custody, they had to rethink their plan.

With a storm building at off the coast, they now planned to wait until nightfall when the marina essentially closed down for the night to move the kids. There was only one-night watchman on duty overnight. An old retired police officer who usually spent his time in the marina office reading detective novels wouldn't be the wiser.

The kids had been drugged during their kidnapping but were awake, tied up and held below deck in the 50-foot Sea Ray.

Polly was confident that their plan had a reasonable chance of success, but there are always unknown factors that could never be accounted for in any mission. She desperately wanted to call the police, but she knew that unless they freed the kids, at this point there was no probable cause for the police to board either craft. All the cops would be looking for was Tom and his involvement in the murders of the Dale and Buffy. She knew she was risking the kids' lives, but after the scene Tom described at Kate's, she knew the kids were collateral damage and would probably be disposed of before morning.

Polly was worried about Tom. He was a scientist and teacher not a special ops agent. Placing a hand on Tom's shoulder, Polly looked into his eyes and said, "Look Tom I know how upset you are. But I have a good plan with a high chance of success. You're just going to have to trust me."

"What our adversaries don't know is that just after sundown, a dense fog will descend on the harbor. That should give us cover from the other boat. Taking out the three men in the Sea Ray should be no problem. And I have a plan for the men in the big boat.

Polly picked up her ship to shore and radioed the Coast Guard that a suspicious boat was docked at the Judith Point Marina. She knew that the Guard was on the lookout for smugglers along the coast and that the black Bahia 100ft superyacht, was exactly the kind of boat they were looking for. She got her friend, Captain Paul Mc Murry on the line and explained that she saw some suspicious men all in black, on a big black boat that looks out of place."

"Yeah, they're parked in the big berth, north of Snug Harbor. Yeah, I thought I saw some weapons on board, so please be careful Paul. No, I'm going to be heading out soon. Uh huh, yeah, ok, well hey thanks Paul. Yeah, I'm doing fine. No, I'm busy again tonight, why don't you give me a call next week. Ok, yeah, the harbor festival sounds like fun. Next week, right? Ok see you then."

Putting down the headset, Polly smiled and said, "Sorry about that Tom. That's my friend Paul, he's a skipper on one the shore patrol boats. He's been wanting to get together for a while now."

"So anyway, the fog should be settling in soon. Once it does, we'll make our move. Don't worry Tom, they won't know what hit them."

Tom was not feeling the confidence that Polly had but he was encouraged by her experience and tenacity. Wearing a whaler's style rain hat he poked his head up through the hatch, and looking ominously at the big superyacht, he said, "Polly I really can't thank you enough for everything you've done. If it wasn't for you, I'd be in jail for murder right now. I'm going to trust your judgement on this and do whatever I can to help, but Polly, I'm a scientist, not a soldier, I used to trap shoot when I was a kid, but I don't even own a gun and I haven't shot one in years."

Polly could sense Tom's reservations, and hugged him as she said, "Tom with any luck it won't come to that, besides, all I have as a couple of flares and a few spear guns. Don't worry. Tom, look, the fog is already starting to come in, let's go over the plan one more time and get ready. Once we rescue the kids, we'll head back to the island. My dad will know what to do."

While the fog thickened in the humid summer night air, Polly put her plan in motion. As they got ready to rescue the kids, Polly started up the huge diesel engines, first to cover any noise they might make boarding the other boat, but also to add to the foggy cover she hoped would aid their mission. She adjusted the choke too rich, adding to the billowing smoke emitted from the twin 1200 horse-power engines.

She had Tom loaded the dart and spear guns and flares into the canvas carryall that she'd brought on board. And as the fog and exhaust from the diesels reached their maximum, she and Tom departed on the port side of the boat opposite their prey. As they quietly moved through the glume of the evening fog, the bellow of the diesels masked their approach. Polly, trying to comfort Tom, whispered in his ear, "Now this will be just like old times, remember when we used to play cops and robbers and shoot each other with those silly rubber dart guns. This is no different. You're going to pretend to be drunk and get in the wrong boat. You know how to do that, I'm sure. Then, when the men below realize there's someone on board they'll come out, I'll shoot them one by one with tranquilizer darts and we rescue the kids. What could go wrong?"

Ok here we go said Tom pulling the whalers cap down over his face, and in his best "had one too many," voices he sang, "In heaven there ain't no beer, that's why we drink it here." Oops whoa," he said as he pretended to slip, as he boarded the sleek craft, "and when we're gone from here…"

One of the men went up onto the cockpit and said, "Hey, what are you doing here?"

Tom drunkenly said, "Whoa- where's my boat?"

Polly perched on the boat landing took aim and shot the man in the neck, he hit the deck before he knew what hit him.

One by one they rose from below deck and met the same fate. In less than 30 seconds, the three attackers were laying helplessly on the cockpit floor.

Tom rushed below to rescue the kids. He found them gagged and bound laying on the v-bunk. Carefully, cutting their ropes and removing their gags, he said, "Now please be quiet, we need to get you out of here."

With the cover of fog and the smoke from the diesel engines, one by one, they were brought up on the dock, and then over to the Polly's racing boat. While Tom secured the kids below, Polly got the boat ready for a quick departure.

Just as they were ready to leave, Captain McMurray could be heard over the Coast Guard shore patrol's loudspeaker. As he maneuvered his 50-foot rigid hull inflatable, behind the super yacht, "A-hoy there, this is Coast Guard Captain Paul Mc Murry. "You there in the black 100-footer, prepare to be boarded."

"Just in time thought Polly," as she revved the engines and slowly backed out of the dock, the huge 1200 horsepower engines quickly pushed the boat out into the breakwater and into the safety of open water.

She brought the boat up on plane then jetted out into the cold waters of the North Atlantic. She throttled up to half speed, until she got out into the bay, still juiced up from the kids rescue, her nerves were just starting to relax. Ten miles from the harbor, she slowed the boat and set the autopilot for Nantucket Island. As Polly went below, she had tears in her eyes as she looked in on Tom and the kids. They were laughing and joking around, exploring the interior of the experimental racing yacht. As she sat on the steps, she watched as Tom interacted with the just released inner city students. Excited by the daring rescue, they kept asking Tom to tell the story of how they were rescued. He just looked on and smiled, and as he looked up and saw Polly crying. He reached up and held her hand and they shared a brief but loving glance.

Tom said above the din, "He kids, this is Polly, she helped rescue us!" The kids, just getting over the shock from their capture and daring rescue, surrounded Polly and started talking all at once.

"How old are you? Are you Tom's girlfriend? Is this your boat? Where are you from? And on and on....

She smiled and said there's plenty of time for questions later. Right now, I need to pilot the boat, Tom, why don't you break out the extra life jackets, there in the forward bin and I'll call dad and see what he thinks we should do now.

While the boat cruised up the coast, Polly use the SAT phone to call her dad. She explained the kidnapping and their daring rescue at the marina. She was sure Tom would be cleared of the murder charges after this, but there were still a few stones left unturned.

She asked her dad to call up to the sheriff's office and have the men in black detained for the kidnapping of Tom's students. Mr. Johnson had considerable pull on the island and had already called his team of attorneys. His main counselor had a house just on the edge of the Johnson property and was already in contact with his friend at the FBI.

She spoke with her dad for several minutes, and they decided the kids could stay at the Johnson estate until arrangements could be made to return them to the city and reunited with their parents.

Of course, the Sheriff and the FBI would want to question Tom, but it could wait till morning. Polly took over the controls and guided the tri-hull racing yacht passed the breakwater and into their private bay.

Still limping from his fall, Tom did the best he could to put the bumpers out and tie off the mooring lines. In the end, she got out to help him, seems Tom didn't know a bowline from a Windsor knot.

The staff at the Johnson mansion was on the doc and welcomed the kids as they stepped out of the boat into the cool Atlantic night air. They were greeted with hugs, large thermos mugs of hot cocoa and warm blankets.

Polly explained the situation to Tom as he limped up the hill toward the house. He was relieved, but understandably upset over the death of his dear friends and concerned about his mother. Kate had proven herself to be very resourceful over the years, but he needed to find her and fast.

He felt that somehow all of this mess was somehow tied to his dad and his research. Tom was never comfortable with the explanation of his father's death. He knew his Mom was hiding something from him and he needed to know the truth.

CHAPTER 8

In the morning, Tom woke to find Polly gone but with a fresh pot of coffee and some pastries on the bedside table to greet him. He slowly got out of bed, took a shower and dressed in the clothes someone had laid out for him. As he made his way downstairs, he could hear a cacophony of laughter coming from the kitchen as the kids attempted to help the chef make breakfast. They were more of a hindrance than a help, but the chef was amused by their curiosity and exuberance.

After a delicious breakfast of fluffy buttermilk pancakes with fresh maple syrup, homemade sausage and farm fresh scrambled eggs, Polly got a call on her cell phone. It was the Sheriff and he asked if it would be okay if he came around the house to interview the kids and take a statement from Tom about what happened yesterday. Polly had already spoken at length with her father and was assured that his attorney would be there during any questioning.

"Yes of course," she said, "that will be fine. What time are you planning on getting here?"

The Sheriff said, "Well, to be honest, we're parked right out in front of the main gate if you don't mind, we like to come in right now."

Polly said, "Well, we are waiting for dad's attorney, but he should be here soon, if you don't mind waiting at the gate."

The sheriff said, "Of course, I fully understand. I just hope he gets here soon; we have a rather large investigation to conduct."

Polly said, "You'll know when he gets here. He'll be coming through the main gate. Please don't follow him right in. Give us about 10 minutes to confer. I'll give you a call when we're ready."

What Polly didn't know, and what the Sheriff didn't disclose, was that right behind his car, was a team of agents from the FBI and CIA. They were very tight-lipped about their involvement in the case. The FBI explained that any kidnapping was a federal matter and run by the FBI but there was no explanation for the presence of the CIA.

A few minutes later, a black SUV pulled up to the main gate which opened upon its arrival and closed again once the car had entered the property. Four men in LL bean hunting attire were escorted out of the car and up the main steps to the large double doors where Mr. Johnson was waiting to greet them. They were brought into Bill's private study where he held a brief meeting before bringing in Tom and Polly.

Phil Collins, Bill Johnson's lead attorney, said, "I'm afraid you caught us just on our way to do some grouse hunting. What's going on Bill that couldn't wait till later?" Bill filled the men in on the situation as they sat in the overstuffed chairs in Bill's well-appointed study. After a minute, Tom and Polly entered the den and stood as the men conferred. Bill was the first to speak, and still standing, went over to Polly, took her hand, lead her and Tom over to a love seat near the fireplace.

Phil, looked at Tom and said, sounds like you've been through a lot. And Miss Polly, how wonderful to see you again, I hear you, always the hero, saved the day again.

As his colleagues looked on, Phil cautioned Tom about disclosing too much information, but said to cooperate fully. Tom was understandably upset and couldn't imagine why anyone would do this.

He said, "I'm just a schoolteacher. If this is about my father's research, I don't know anything? My class is doing a research project on climate change, but my kids are just in high school. Our research methods are really not all that sophisticated."

Tom left out the part about stumbling on some of his father's old research papers in an obscure online scientific journal.

Sitting forward on the couch, Tom said, "Now that the kids are safe, I really need to find my mother Kate. She called me before we left school yesterday afternoon. She sounded a little out of sorts, but I wasn't able to talk to her. After I got to the island and I found the Joneses murdered, I searched the house, but she was gone. I saw that someone had ransacked my dad's old office looking for something. And I know I should have stayed behind but I was afraid I was being set up. So, I planned to escape in the ultra-light but found it gone. That's when I made my way to the Johnson House and found Polly at the dock, and with her help, we were able to find the kidnappers and free the kids, but I've got no idea where my mom went."

Phil stood, and as he walked around the ornate conference table said, "Maybe the Sheriff can shed some light on her disappearance. Flying in a craft that small, she's probably still on the island and if she thought she was in danger she may be hiding out at a friend's."

He walked over and pulled a chair closer to where Tom and Polly were sitting. He looked Tom in the eye and said, "We don't think you're going to be charged with anything at this time, but they're definitely going to have some serious questions for you about the kidnapping of the kids and murder of your mom's caretakers. It's fairly obvious that you had nothing to do with either the kidnapping or the murder, but they are going to want to question you anyway. So just answer their questions truthfully. You really have nothing to hide and what we don't want, is for you to be hit with an obstruction of justice charge. So, unless you have any questions, we're going to let them in and get this over with.

Polly called the sheriff on her cell phone and as both cars entered the property, the gate was closed behind them. They were greeted at the door by Mr. Johnson and lead into the expansive formal dining room, where Tom, Polly, and Mr. Johnson's attorneys were already seated at the large antique table. The Sheriff's came in and were well known to Mr. Johnson and Polly. The four men dressed in dark suits just walked in without saying anything and stood against the wall.

The sheriff started first, directing his questions at Tom and said, "Tom, we understand you've been through a lot, but we just have a few questions to ask. We have a team from county social services, that's going to be coming along shortly to interview the kids and return them to their parents. We just wanted to get your story here. So, if you can, sort of give us a rundown of what happened leading up to your departure from the school and what happened during the events that led up to the kidnapping and murder of your mother's caretaker's."

Tom looked around the room nervously. He knew the Sheriff since he was a kid. Two of the men leaning against the wall were dressed in bad suits and looked like your typical FBI agents. The other two men were introduced as federal agents. They were tall and lean and well-dressed, wearing Armani suits with military style haircuts and just didn't fit in somehow. They had the x-military look of the men that chased Tom and the kids through the city yesterday and he cautiously eyed them up and down.

Tom looked the Sheriff in the eye and said, "I am fully prepared to cooperate in any way that I can. I just want to understand what really happened yesterday. But now that everyone is safe, my first concern is the whereabouts of my mother Kate. I'm assuming that she was in some way threatened by the people who murdered the Joneses and escaped. So, I'm just asking if there's been any word from her or if anyone has any information about where she might be?"

The sheriff looked at Tom and said, "We are just as baffled about her disappearance as you are son. We've had no word from her at all. Now, we are conducting a house by house search on any property big enough to land an ultralight, but we've been told they can land just about anywhere. She may have landed on Chappaquiddick or Martha's Vineyard, and we're checking, but haven't found anything yet. I promise you Tom; will you'll be the first one to know as soon as we hear anything."

Tom, sitting next to Polly, reached out and held her hand and looked down at the floor as he started to recount the events of the previous day. Never looking up, he told his story, starting with the text messages he got from Yia, and the chase through the streets of New York City. The deputies recorded his statement on a small voice recorder and the suits, now sitting at the far end of the table, just listened quietly occasionally taking notes on a small pocket notepads. He finished by recounting Polly's daring rescue of the kids, and he as he looked up, he said, "That's everything I can remember."

The sheriff looked at Polly and asked if she had anything to add that Tom may have left out during the time that he was with her. Still gently holding Tom's hand, she shook her head and said, "No that's about it, as I remember."

The Sheriff said, "Ok then, we want to thank you for your time. We're going to need to get in touch with you if we have any further questions, but for right now, we're just going to ask you not to leave the country without letting us know. Thank you again for your cooperation. We're going to go back to the office and file our paperwork. These gentlemen from the federal government would like to have an additional word with you."

The Sheriff deputies got up to leave and Mr. Johnson escorted them out the front door. Meanwhile, the four feds remained seated at the table.

One of the FBI agents spoke first, introducing himself and his colleague, and nodding towards the other two men and explained that they were with a 911 task force.

He commended Polly on her daring rescue of the students at the marina. Then he said, "We need to have some confidential discussions with Mr. Loveton, so we have to ask you to leave at this time.

And looking at Mr. Johnson's four attorneys he nodded to his associate and he took out a red folder and handed an official-looking document to one of the attorneys. He read it and passed it along to the other three. They got up and had a short discussion before going to Mr. Johnson and explaining that under court order, the discussion they are about to have with Tom has been deemed top secret. Tom could refuse to answer questions but according to this document signed by Circuit Court Judge Rudolph. Unless he cooperates, he could be brought into custody.

Mr. Johnson thought to himself, "*What the hell has Tom gotten himself into now.*"

Tom excused himself to go to the bathroom and one of the agents insisted on escorting him there and back. Tom returned to the dining room with more questions than he had answers, but he was determined to get to the bottom of what exactly what happened and who was responsible.

They directed Tom to sit in the middle of the large antique banquet table, while the other two men took out some sort of scanners and were searching the room for listening devices. Tom thought this was a ridiculous precaution to take to interview a simple schoolteacher, but they obviously thought otherwise.

Drawing the curtains and turning on the lights, they gathered around Tom as he shifted nervously in his seat. One of the FBI agents spoke first, and he said, "The men at the marina were apprehended. We are still checking on their background, but they appear to be pros. Mercenaries. Guns for hire. Call them what you will. We have reason to believe these men are connected to an industrial espionage group linked to extortion, attempted coups, and murder-for-hire. We don't know who hired them, but we're working on it. Tom, these are some really bad men. We're still not sure what their plan was. We think that they kidnapped the kids to be used as leverage and killed the Jones to frame you, but that's just a theory at this point.

Tom said, "Now wait a minute. I've given this a lot of thought, and I'm no detective, but there was no way to know that we were on our way to the island. I got a call from Kate just before we left the school. But at that time, I had no idea where we were going. You might want to rethink your scenario about what happened. It looks to me like two different teams from the same group tried to kidnap us, and at the same time, another team went to the island and we just happened the end up at Nana's by accident."

The agent said, "You know Tom, at this point we're still gathering all the facts. We have to assume the two groups were working together and when you left the dock there was a good possibility that you were heading to your mother's. Our working theory is that they called the other team to let them know you might be on your way."

With a strong feeling of exasperation in his voice Tom said, "The caretakers and dogs were dead before I got there. There is no way that the team in the city could have got their before we did."

One of the FBI agents approached Tom and said, "There is a lot about this case that we don't know yet. There may have been multiple teams, they may have used a helicopter. We just don't know at this time. One thing we do know, is that due to the heavy traffic in and around New York City, the fastest way to travel up and down the coast is by speed boat." Then as he circled the table, he said, "Anyway, let's move on. I know that you must have a lot of questions.

We are reasonably certain that this case has something to do with your father."

Tom said, "But my father died in a car crash 20 years ago. I know he was involved in some controversial research, but why would anyone go to this length, 20 years after his death, to kidnap a classroom full of kids and murder two innocent people. I don't know anything about my father's research. I'm just a simple high school teacher."

The man said, "Tom, we know this is going to be hard for you to understand, but your father is not dead. In fact, we believe he faked his death to get away from the same people or organization that was after you and the kids yesterday."

Tom was getting frustrated at this point and he tried to stand but was pushed forcefully back into his chair. He looked incredulously at the four men and said, "Well if my father is still alive then where the hell is he?"

The agent backed off and said, "Tom, these other two men are actually from the NSA. Apparently, they've been tracking your father's activities for several years now." He stood as he said, "I'm going to let them fill you in on the details."

The two men got up to sit closer. One of them poured a glass of water from a crystal pitcher on the table and handed it to Tom. As they sat down, one of the men, looking at the FBI agents said, "I'm sorry, but I'm going to have to ask the two of you to leave. National security, you don't have clearance."

The agents gave him a look and one of them said, "Hey, come on guys, we're all on the same team here."

The man just looked at him and said, "Call your boss if you have any questions, but I have my orders."

The two FBI agents, surprised by the request, grabbed their stuff and said on their way out, "We'll be waiting outside."

The closest one introduced himself as Todd Rundgren from the CIA. He pulled out a folder marked top secret and said, "Now I know Tom, this is going to be hard to believe, but your dad is alive and well and has been living in New Zealand all this time. I know it sounds crazy, but we believe that your father faked his death and went into hiding after death threats were made against the family for the controversial reports that he published regarding man-made climate change."

"Tom, we understand that without verifiable proof you can't just take our word for it. And we're sorry for holding back this information from you all this time, but it was a matter of National Security."

"I can tell you that we've had your father under surveillance for several years. Actually, several decades. At first, we didn't think much about what he was doing but then things started to change. The New Zealand government once a US ally, began to distance themselves from US involvement. Originally, we thought that peculiar but nothing to really worry about. So, we just watched and waited. Then about 10 years ago we started observing some strange things going on in a factory in the interior of the country that we think your father built on an old sheep farm. I have some high-resolution satellite photos that were taken recently that may help illustrate our point."

As he laid the photos out on the table, he said, "As you can see here, when you look closer, you can see the magnitude of the complex that he designed and built. It covers an area of over 8 football fields in size. According to our sources, they have been quietly sourcing materials from China. The extent of their relationship is unclear. In addition, through advances in technology, he has found a way to mine deep underground for rare earth minerals and essential elements to build high-tech machinery.

"We have gone to great lengths to infiltrate his facilities with no success. It appears he has the full cooperation of the New Zealand government. In fact, we have reason to believe that he is financing the New Zealand government and may have taken control of the government itself or at least he's paying them to cooperate with his production facilities."

"As he pulled out another folder and set it on the table he said, "Our intelligence indicates that your father has constructed one of the largest factories in the world. As you can see from these photos, the factory is camouflaged extremely well and to the naked eye blends into the natural surroundings. So, for years most of it went undetected."

"But then things started to change. One of our Southeastern Pacific satellites started having problems and then stopped communicating altogether with ground control. At first, we thought it was just a malfunction. Further analysis of the satellites internal coding system showed that the unit had been taken over. We thought it was the Chinese due to the close proximity to the Chinese mainland. Then we intercepted a stream of microwave messages emanating from a Satellite facility on a deserted island off the North coast of New Zealand."

He said, "Tom, these photos are classified to the highest level. Your father is a brilliant man and should not be underestimated. We have intercepted some of your father's communication and correspondence with other scientists around the world, and if our suspicions are correct your father has built the largest robotic factory in the world on an island off the North coast of New Zealand. We have reached out to the New Zealand government through diplomatic channels and have been stonewalled at every turn. No one goes into this facility and no one ever goes out. Even the factory supply ships are met at the harbor and all shipping containers are transferred via their own fleet and brought into the factory independently. So, like I said no one goes in and no one goes out."

"But obviously we're not the only ones interested in your father's research and factory output. We believe this is why your students were kidnapped and the Jones' killed while trying to capture your mother. We believe that whoever was pulling the strings behind this operation intended to blackmail your father. Blackmail him for what, we don't know. Cases like this usually are about trade secrets, and corporate espionage. It seems that your father has made some amazing advances in technology. Any time you do that you become a target for corporate espionage. In addition, the oil and coal industries are just as powerful when your father went into hiding. Some of these organizations will stop at nothing to get what they want."

Tom took a few moments to absorb what they were telling him. He took a couple of sips from his glass of water, got up from his chair and started walking around the table. As he was pacing back and forth, he said, "So you're telling me, and you expect me to believe that my father, who died in a car crash 20 years ago. Actually, escaped to New Zealand, where he built a secret factory, making robots. Wow, I don't know where you guys come up with this stuff. Unless you have some kind of proof other than these satellite photos, how the hell am I supposed to believe you.

The agent got up turned around and leaned on the dining room table facing Tom and as the other agent drew in closer said, "I can truly understand how you feel Tom. If the situation was reversed, I'm sure I would feel the same way. And I'm sorry about this, but we have a court order to take you into protective custody. After what happened yesterday, I think you can understand it's for your own protection." He then pulled out an official looking court document to show Tom that he was to be remanded into the custody of the CIA.

Tom looked at the document and was speechless. He stammered and managed to say, "May I confer with an attorney."

The agent just smiled and looking at Tom said, "I really wish you could, but under the circumstances this situation falls under the Patriot Act. The only people that can be briefed on this must have a "top secret" security clearance. This order is signed by Judge Rudolph, part of the Homeland Security Task Force and the assistant attorney general.

As he started to put the files back in the folder he said, "A lot of the details I can't go into because they're top secret. So, if you'll just come with us, we have a jet on the tarmac at the airport here in Nantucket. Tom, I know you want to say your goodbyes to Polly and the kids, but we really have to get going as soon as possible."

He continued by saying, "Once we get you into protective custody, we can have you speak with someone from the US Attorney's office. You can go willingly or in handcuffs, but one way or another you're coming with us."

Tom sheepishly said, "Okay, I get your point, let me just talk to Polly and say goodbye to the kids and we can be on our way."

Just then there was a knock at the door and Polly peaked her head inside and said, "Are you guys finished yet? Social services are here to pick up the kids and they're just getting ready to leave." Looking at Tom she said, "I thought you'd want to say goodbye."

The agent looked at Tom and said, "As I said before, I'm sure you want to say your goodbyes but make it quick."

A little flustered, Tom looked at Polly and said, "I'll be right there."

As he walked towards the door, he said, "Well if you›ll excuse me for a few minutes. I›d like to see the kids off." Polly was waiting for him on the other side of the door, took his hand and lead him into the foray, where the kids were preparing to leave. As Tom approached, almost in unison several kids said, "Mr. Loveton are you coming with us?"

Doing his best to muster a smile he looked at them and said, "No, I won't be coming with you but I'm sure you're in good hands."

Tom walked with Polly outside as the kids were led into a large passenger van. He said as he shut the van door, "We are going to have to suspend school for a few days, but I'll see you all very soon have a safe trip back to the city."

Holding hands, Tom and Polly watched and waved as the van slowly made its way up the long driveway and as the gate opened several of the kids looked through the back window and waved goodbye. Polly gave Tom a hug and whispered in his ear that her dad wanted to talk to him.

Together they went up the steps and through the large main double doors and into Mr. Johnson's private study. One of the agents wanted to follow them inside, but Mr. Johnson, a man used to getting what he wanted, held him back and said, "Can we have a little privacy please? It will be just a moment." And he ushered Polly and Tom into the room and locked the door.

Cautiously the agent stepped back and said, "Okay, I'll be waiting right out here."

As they entered the study, Mr. Johnson's attorneys were seated at a round table and one of them stood as they entered. Tom and Polly made themselves comfortable in a love-seat next to the fireplace while Mr. Johnson took a single wingback chair opposite them and the attorneys came over and sat on the couch. Tom told them that he was required to go with the agents against his will and that they said it was a matter of National Security.

Bill got up and turned on an old classic stereo system. As traditional jazz played in the background he said," Hopefully this will prevent any eavesdroppers." He returned to his seat and said to Tom,

"We are not sure that those men are who they say they are. In the document they presented, there were a couple of red flags. First of all, Judge Rudolph retired last month, so unless they drew those documents up in advance of this event, it doesn't seem likely that the document is genuine. That being said, we suspect that one or more of the men maybe imposters."

It›s too bad the sheriff deputies aren›t here to help us sort this out, but I›m afraid you might be in grave danger. We have a plan that will help you escape but we›ve got to be very careful."

Mr. Johnson looked at Tom and laid out their plan. Tom was impressed by the well thought out plan and suspected that Polly had a major role in the details. When Mr. Johnson was finished, he looked at Polly, smiled and said," Alright, everyone clear on the plan?" Everyone nodded in silence as the gravity of what they are about to do became all too real.

As planned, the attorneys got up and went out to their SUV and left the estate. Mr. Johnson went upstairs, and Tom followed Polly into the kitchen to get something to eat. The agent waiting outside the study door followed them into the kitchen and said to Tom, "If you have any personal things to take with you let's get them now."

Tom looked at the agent and said, "I came here with the clothes on my back, so I've got nothing to take. If it's okay with you, we're going to have a quick lunch. I will need to go to the bathroom, and I'll be ready to go. Casually looking at the agent he said, "You want anything to eat?"

Polly was making a couple of sandwiches, and Tom went to the bay window and looked towards the breakwater. As he thought over the plan, he thought to himself, "*If we're lucky it might just work.*"

Polly was finishing up the sandwiches and asked Tom if he wanted potato salad or coleslaw. He said, "I'll have whatever you're having, and he said, "Hey Pol, you got any soda?"

She said, "Sure, the sodas in the fridge over by the pantry, help yourself. I'll meet you at the table by the window."

Tom said, "Do you want one?"

Polly smiled and said, "No thanks, I'm just having some water." Under the watchful eye of the CIA agent, they sat at the table near the bay window and ate their sandwiches in uncomfortable silence. Feeling somewhat awkward, Polly said, "The kids seemed to be in good spirits considering."

Tom said, "Yeah growing up in the city, those kids have really seen a lot, they're pretty resilient." As Tom finished the last bite of his sandwich, he stood up and said, "Well I've got to get going so I guess this is goodbye. Polly stood up and under the watchful eye of the agent, gave him a warm embrace and slipped a small flashlight into his pocket and whispered in his ear, "Remember Tom, the handle on the toilet still sticks like it always has."

Tom looked Polly in the eye gave her a little wink as he smiled as he said, "We'll have to do this again soon." Then looking at the agent he said, "I'll be ready to go in just a minute, I have to use the facilities."

Polly looked at Tom and said, "You remember where the downstairs bathroom is don't you?" Tom looked at her and said, "It's still under the back stairs isn't it?"

Polly laughed and said, "Yes silly, it's still there." Then as she turned her back towards the agent she said as she handed Tom a custom Johnson Racing Team hat, "Here Tom, don't forget your hat. You're an honorary member of the racing team now don't forget that." And as she headed out of the kitchen she said, "I'm going to go check on Dad, I'll meet you out front in a couple minutes."

The agent followed Tom down the hallway towards the bathroom under the back stairs. He opened the door and checked inside and said, "Don't take too long in there we have a schedule to keep."

Tom entered the interior of the small bathroom and looked for the hidden passageway behind the sidewall. It was right where he remembered. He went back to the toilet and wanting to be as convincing as possible, took his time doing his business and flushed. He ran water in the sink and washed his hands. Sure enough, the old toilet had never been fixed after all these years and the handle stuck making a whining sound as water running through the old pipes groaned in protest and made the perfect cover for his escape.

The main part of the Johnson House dated back over 300 years and was used by smugglers when pirates still roamed the high seas. Tom slowly opened the small bathroom window as a decoy then he carefully closed the panel behind him and using the small flashlight Polly had slipped into his pocket, he open the hidden door and made his way carefully down the winding staircase into the dingy basement. His memory of this part of the house was vague but Polly instructed him to go to the north east corner and search for the large iron door still on its original rollers concealing an underground passageway to the boathouse.

Meanwhile, as part of the plan, Mr. Johnson went upstairs to his bedroom, and did his best to match the clothing that Tom was wearing. And before leaving his room, he donned a Johnson Team racing hat just like the one Polly had given Tom in the kitchen. He snuck down the back stairway and into the 6-car garage and got behind the wheel of his black supercharged Land Rover. He inserted his cell phone to the dashboard charger and waited for Polly's text.

As the groan of the toilet, began to fade, the agent still covering the bathroom door grew impatient. He knocked on the door and said, "Time to go Mr. Loveton. We've got a plane to catch."

Thankful that Polly had the foresight to provide him with a flashlight, Tom searched the dark basement until he found the old wrought iron door concealing the underground tunnel to the boathouse. He slid the heavy door on its rollers and peered into the dark cavern, anxiously waiting for Polly to arrive. Polly went down the back stairway into the dingy basement and made her way to the north east corner to meet Tom. She arrived just as Tom was stepping into the dank confines of the old tunnel. Using hand gestures, Polly motioned Tom to enter the tunnel and they both slid the door closed behind them.

Polly quickly gave Tom a nervous hug and motioned for them to continue through the tunnel to the boathouse. Tom's ankle was still sore from his fall the day before and he struggled to balance himself on the slippery stone floor. Polly looked back at Tom's progress and said, "I'll go up ahead and get the boat ready. I'll leave the hatch to the boathouse open, so just climb up the ladder and close the hatch behind you. I'll meet you out at the dock." Tom just nodded and holding the sides of the tunnel, made his way as quickly as he could.

The agent at the bathroom door grew more impatient and started forcefully knocking on the door and yelling for Tom. He tried the door and found it locked. He radioed to the other agent and said, "We have a problem, Loveton is in the bathroom with the door locked and is not responding."

By this time Polly had made her way through the tunnel, up the ladder and through the hatch into the boathouse where she took out her cell phone and sent a pre-recorded text to her father waiting in the garage. With a slight grin, he started up the 5.6-liter super-charged V8 engine, opened the garage door and made a rapid it exit towards the main gate. The other agents, assuming it was Tom trying to escape, radioed to each other and said, "Loveton is escaping in the Land Rover and heading for the main gate, we're going to pursue." The agent by the bathroom door, took out his Glock 9 and shot the lock on the door, splintering the aged wood, and forcing the door open, saw the open window and realized, Tom had escaped. Without taking time investigate further, he ran towards the front where the other agents were just getting into the black rental SUV. He ran down the hall towards the front door and as he shouldered his Glock, closed the passenger side door as they raced up the long driveway towards the street. The NSA agent quickly took out his phone and sent a text message as they gave chase.

By this time, Tom had made his way through the tunnel and up the ladder to the boat house. As he stepped out onto the main dock, Polly had already cast off the mooring lines and was just getting the engines primed and ready for a quick departure. While the agents sent to collect Tom were chasing the Land Rover, Tom and Polly were making their second escape in as many days.

Tom, gingerly went below, got a life jacket and a helmet and came up to the cockpit just as Polly was about to start the engines. Polly looked at Tom and said," So far so good, let's get the hell out of here."

Polly started the twin diesel engines with a roar, and they made their way out of the small harbor through the breakwater and out into the open ocean where she pushed down the throttle controls and opened up the sleek racing yacht to almost full power. They made their way up the coast towards City Point Harbor, where Captain McMurray, would be waiting for them.

Meanwhile, the attorneys had a surprise waiting for the agents as Mr. Johnson, racing down the single lane dirt road, lead them through the woods and bramble. Mr. Collins, Johnson's lead attorney had a hunting shack just on the edge of the Johnson estate and when they left the house, set an ambush. Mr. Johnson's Range Rover far out matched the standard rental SUV and made it into the circle drive of the shack well ahead of the slower car.

As he entered the driveway, he swerved, just in front of the house placing the car perpendicular to the gate. Collins and his team already had their shotguns loaded and were strategically located, taking cover behind trees and outbuildings on the edge of the drive. Collins handed Mr. Johnson a hunting rifle and they hid behind the Range Rover. As the agents skidded to a stop, they expected to see Tom making his way towards the shack but when they got out of the car with their guns drawn, they were surprised by 5 well-armed men pointing high powered rifles at them. Collins took the lead and simply said, "Drop your guns or we'll shoot." Not prepared for a gunfight, the agents dropped their pistols and put their hands in the air.

Collins had called the Sheriff's office just as they left the Johnson property and the sheriff's men were already on their way to the shack. Collins, a Marine Corps veteran said in a commanding tone, "Get on the ground face down with your hands clasped behind your neck." The agents reluctantly complied just as the sheriff arrived with a team of deputies.

The Sheriff said as he got out of the car, "Nice work boys, something didn't seem right about a couple of those guys. One of the agents on the ground said, "you're making a huge mistake. I'm with the FBI check my ID. We are in pursuit of an escaped prisoner and you are facing charges of obstruction of justice."

Mr. Collins walked up to the agent and said, "Is that so? You might be with the FBI, but what about these two other fellas, that court order that they showed us is as phony as a $3 bill. Judge Rudolph retired last month, so how could he have written out an order this morning?"

The agent said, I don't know about the other two, they joined us at the airport, said they were NSA with a 911 task force and assigned to the case. They showed us their IDs, so we let them come along, that's all I know."

The Sheriff said as the men were being cuffed and forcefully moved into the back of a sheriff's van. "We'll sort all that out back at the station. For now, you boys just make yourself comfortable and we'll get to the bottom of this back at the office."

After receiving a text message from the back of the rental car, the pilot of a black military style helicopters, took off from a clearing, just on the edge of the Johnson estate, and raced just above the tree line towards the breakwater. The bright yellow, racing boat was an easy target in the bright mid-day sun of the Atlantic coast.

Thinking they were out of danger, Polly pulled back on the throttles and let the boat drift in the slight northerly current. Taking off her helmet she said, "Wow that went off without a hitch."

Tom took off his helmet and using his hand to shield his eyes from the bright sun he said, "That was a great plan. Do I get a two-for-one discount on rescues now?"

Polly laughed and said, "We're not in the clear yet. I'd rather be safe than sorry. If any of those guys were connected to the men that killed the Joneses and kidnapped the kids, we still have to be very careful. It was a good thing my dad had his attorney to check the court documents or you might be in their custody by now."

Polly said, "I just need to check with my dad, and we'll be on our way. She got out her sat phone and speed dialed her dad's cell phone. He answered on the first ring and said, "Did you guys make it out okay?" Smiling and giving Tom a thumbs up, she said, "Yeah the plan went perfectly on this end, what about you?

On the other end, he said, "They never knew what hit them until it was too late. The Sheriffs are just taking them in right now and I'm going back to the house. Are you on your way to meet Captain McMurray?"

"Yes," she said, "I just wanted to check with you first. We'll be underway soon; I'll call you from the City Point Dock."

Bill said, "Okay, be careful. There's a lot more going on here then we know."

Just then, Polly heard the unmistakable roar of a helicopter fast approaching from the south. She grabbed her marine binoculars and saw a black military style helicopter approaching fast, just skimming the water, heading right for her boat. She yelled to Tom, "Get your gear back on quick, we've got company. Pulling on her racing helmet, she revved the big engines and raced towards shore.

Her boat was fast but was no match for the helicopter which was about 5 miles off their stern. Thinking quickly, she had Tom take the controls and said through the helmet com link, "Just hold her steady at this heading. I have to go below for a second. Tom, a skilled sailor and yachtsman, took the controls and looked in the rearview mirror at the approaching helicopter. What seemed to him like forever was actually only about 30 seconds, when Polly appeared with a large harpoon gun and a bag of coiled wire.

She said as she opened the bag and attached the clasp for the wire to the whaling harpoon, "They're going to be on us in about 90 seconds. I'm assuming our new friends aren't here on a sightseeing expedition."

Just then, high caliber machine gun bullets were strafing the ocean water around the boat. The hull was composed of high-strength carbon fiber and was virtually bulletproof, unfortunately their life vests and helmets were not.

Polly reached over and adjusted the throttle slowing the craft by just a few knots. She said to Tom, "Stay on this heading. When they get close, I'm going to use the harpoon to try to bring them down, but we've only got one shot at this." Tom gave her a little salute and said to her, "If anyone can do it Lieutenant Johnson, you're the one."

She said to Tom, "When I say now, drop down to 1/2 speed and turn hard to starboard."

She said, "Ok let's get rid of these assholes." Polly went to the stern and steadied herself for the shot. The helicopter was now within about 50 yards. The helicopter had the side door open and we're still shooting, around the boat, but with the turbulence in the air and water they were not well positioned to take out the engines. Polly waited until the last moment and yelled into her microphone, now! Tom pulled back on the throttle and spun the wheel to starboard and the boat dug into the water and made a 90-degree turn just as the helicopter was getting in position. Polly brought the harpoon gun up to her shoulder, took aim and fired. The big gun used for tagging blue whales, sounded like a cannon going off as the harpoon was launched high into the air just in front of the helicopter with the steel cable in tow.

As with any improvised plan, it was Polly's experience that luck always played a significant role and luck was on Polly's side. Just as she fired, the helicopter swooped down to just above the water and turning to the left, angled the open door towards the boat. The harpoon just missed the fuselage as it hit just above the rotor. The cable tangled itself in the rotor shaft, and in seconds, the helicopter's steel cable, caught the spinning titanium blades, cutting the fuselage into a dozen pieces as what was left of the craft, crashed into the water just 50 yards from the racing boat.

Tom pulled back on the throttle and turned the boat to face the crash. Polly looked at the crash site and then at Tom and she said, "Tom, that was no ordinary helicopter."

Removing his helmet, he looked at her and said, "Yeah no shit, that one was trying to kill us."

"No, Tom that's not what I meant," Polly said as she motored over to the crash site.

The main part of the cabin was still afloat as they approached, and she said, "See the markings on the side? Like I said, that's no ordinary helicopter."

Looking down at the slowly sinking wreckage, Tom said, "What exactly do you mean Pol?

With a look that could melt steel she said, "That's a black ops military bird. I flew in the navy version when I was in the core. The only people authorized to fly that kind of craft are US military or US military contractors."

Tom looked at her and said, "What are you saying Polly? The government is trying to kill us?"

As Polly throttled up heading for the City Point dock, she said, "That's exactly what I'm saying Tom. We are in some deep shit. They are probably looking at us right now."

Tom got out the marine binoculars and scanned the horizon.

Polly said, "No stupid, from space. A bird in the sky, you know, a spy satellite."

Starting to panic he said, "What the fuck are we going to do now?"

She said as she said, "Strap yourself in, and don't worry I've got a plan."

CHAPTER 9

Polly radioed Captain McMurry over the ship to shore radio on a special band assigned to navy operations and spoke briefly to her friend Paul over the headset wired to the cockpit.

Tom, still wearing his racing helmet, sat in the stern and just stared out at the expansive ocean.

His thoughts went to his mother and just where she might be, when Polly abruptly restarted the engines and said as she donned her helmet said, "Come on Tom, strap in, we need to get to port asap!"

Polly was really worried at this point; she couldn't understand why a black ops military contractor would have a team out after Tom.

Tom was beside himself with worry. He just learned that his father who he thought died in a car accident 20 years ago was alive and living in New Zealand. He still had no idea where his Mother was.

Polly radioed ahead to Captain McMurray who had his Coast Guard Patrol boat waiting for her at the City Point dock. Driving her racing boat like the hounds of hell were on their trail, Polly entered the harbor and spoke with Captain McMurray over her encrypted SAT phone. She guided her boat passed the breakwater and took a slip a few spaces away where the Coast Guard Patrol boat was docked. The dock crew was waiting for her and helped tie off the sleek racing yacht. Tom, getting used to the routine, pulled the bumpers out of the racks and tied them off over the side. Polly turned and said, "Tom let's go below for a minute we need to make a quick change."

Tom removed his helmet and life vest, while Polly rummage through a cabinet and tossed Tom a Johnson Racing Team jumpsuit, windbreaker and a broad-brimmed sun hat. As she changed into her racing team jumpsuit, she said, "We've got to make this quick, hurry and put these on. I'm sure there's another team on the mainland looking for us right now." She grabbed a hat and a windbreaker just like the one she gave to Tom and said," Captain McMurray's waiting for us. We'll be safe once we get on board, but first I need to see the harbormaster. Let's go!"

Once the boat was tied off, Polly left the keys with one the attendants and as they made their way to the harbormaster's office. She quickly explained her plan to Tom as they avoided the spray coming up through the dock as a group of joy riders ignored the "slow-no-wake" signs and water splashed up through wooden slats of the old dock.

Once in the office, Polly took off her jacket and hat and had Tom do the same. Two of Captain McMurry's crew were waiting for them in the office. One, a handsome young man about Tom's size, and the other, a tall athletic blonde. They quickly removed their baseball style hats and coastguard jackets and handed them to Polly. Polly set them down on the coffee table in the cramped office and said as she unzipped her jumpsuit, "Ok, everybody strip." The astonished coast guard crew just stood there, and Polly said, "That's an order."

They quickly complied as they removed their coast guard uniforms and tried not to smirk as they stood there in their skivvies in front of the harbor master and two complete strangers. Polly handed over her jumpsuit as Tom did the same. They all switched clothes as a befuddled harbormaster pretended to shuffle some papers on his desk as tried not to look at the four near naked sailors in his office. With the coastguard crew, now wearing a set of Johnson Racing Team apparel, they quickly left the office, and Polly said, "I left the keys with the dock crew, be careful." Not fully knowing what they were getting into, the two crew members walked down to the racing boat and quickly started the engines. And as the dock crew untied the mooring lines and threw the dock bumpers on board, they waved as the boat raced out of the harbor and headed out to sea.

Now dressed in official coast guard uniforms, Tom and Polly left the office and slowly made their way towards the coast guard cutter where Captain McMurry was waiting. As Tom and Polly walked across the gangplank, Captain McMurray ordered his crew to make-way.

Once on board, Tom and Polly were ushered below while the crew prepared for a quick departure. Captain McMurray came below, had a few quick words with Polly and then went back up to the Pilot House.

The engines started, and the ship cast off and headed towards the breakwater. While Tom was shown the way to the head, Polly followed the captain topside, where she had a few quick words with the former Seal Team Commander. As he navigated the busy shipping channel, Polly went below. She found Tom casually chatting with a cute midshipman, or midship-women as it were. Polly gave her a stern look and said, "Would you excuse us?" Guiding Tom to a couch in the officers lounge and sitting in a chair next to him she said, "Tom I know you've been through a lot the last couple days, don't worry, we'll be safe here. Hopefully, we can find out what's going on. Captain McMurray has some contacts in the NSA he should be able to shed some light on our situation. He should be down here soon."

After the attack and destruction of the helicopter, Tom was in shock. He still couldn't believe what happened at his Mother's house. Kidnapping the kids was one thing, but the murder of two innocent people was another. That combined with the attack from the helicopter was just too much for Tom to comprehend. Polly could tell by the look on Tom's face that confronting him with the current situation would just make matters worse. She fixed him a cup of tea and handing it to him said, "I'll be right back, I'm going to go have a few words with the captain."

She was on her way up to the bridge as Captain McMurray was heading below. They practically bumped into each other on the stairway and Polly said, "Tom's not doing too well. I think he's in shock. Is there somewhere private we can talk?"

Captain McMurray looked cautiously at his old friend, he mustered a smile and said, "Yes of course the map room is right this way," and he led her downstairs and through the narrow hallway towards the stern. He opened the steel bulkhead door and motioned for Polly to have a seat at the center table. A large port side window illuminated the small room and provided them with a view of the open water as they headed out to sea.

There was an uncomfortable silence as Captain McMurry poured a glass of water from a stainless-steel pitcher, magnetically held in place on the steel table and handing Polly a glass settled into a chair bolted to the floor. They both spoke at the same time, and Polly said, "Excuse me Captain you were going to say something?"

He looked at her and said, "I was concerned when I got your radio call, is this something to do with the helicopter crash I heard over the radio."

Polly was hoping that the chase and subsequent crash had gone unnoticed. She said, "Yes that's partly why we're here. It seems my friend Tom has some powerful enemies. I don't know if they're trying to capture or kill him, but that was no ordinary helicopter that crashed and sunk off the coast."

Captain McMurray said, "The crash was reported on an emergency channel buy a passing fishing trawler. We have a salvage team in route to the reported crash site right now if there's anything you can tell me it might help."

Draining the water glass, Polly said," Do you have anything stronger? I could use real drink." Captain McMurry, gave her a look and opening a small cabinet took out a bottle of 15-year-old scotch. He took her empty water glass and gave her a generous pour.

Taking a big gulp from of fiery liquid she said, "Ok let's talk, but this is strictly off the record?"

The captain gave her a stern look and said, "What the hell's going on Polly."

Getting up from her seat and walking towards the window, she turned and said, "I was hoping you could help us fill in the blanks."

Captain McMurray saw the frightened look in Polly's face and said, "You know Polly, we go back a long way, and I'll do whatever I can for you. Why don't you fill me in on what you know so far? Grabbing a hand-held radio from the table he spoke briefly to his XO and turning the Polly said, "Why don't you have a seat and tell me what's going on."

Still pacing the floor, Polly recounted the recent events; the kidnapping and murder of the caretakers, Kates escape in the ultralight, their narrow escape from the Johnson estate and the helicopter attack.

Captain McMurry, was taking notes on an iPad as she went through the details of the last 2 days. When she finished, he said, "The two of you have had a rough couple of days, I can see why a "civi" like Tom is in such bad shape. We are trained to deal with situations like this but a professor? Polly, let me ask you a question. Why come to me? Why not go to the police?"

Polly shifted in her seat and said, "Whatever is going on here is deeper than anything the local police can do. We can't just sit around and watch a bunch of incompetent bureaucrats twiddle their thumbs. That wasn't just any helicopter, Paul. I need to reach out to your friends at the NSA if you can."

Having made up his mind Captain McMurray said, "I'll make some calls. In the meantime, we've got to find a safe place for you to hide. You obviously can't stay here, why don't you join Tom in the lounge, and I'll see what I can do."

Polly found Tom out on the fly bridge, watching a flock of seagulls following the ship's wake. She said, "The Captain has agreed to help us for now. But we have to find a safe place to hide out until we can sort out this mess. I'm just afraid any calls we make could be monitored. Do you have any ideas?"

Tom turned to face her and said, "My family has a farm in upper NY state. It's in the Adirondacks, the middle of nowhere. We could hide out there for a while, but I haven't been there in years. I don't even know the address, but I'm sure I could find it on a map, it's just south of Roman's Nose. Kate goes there every year for the fall colors."

Polly said, "I suppose we could rent a car, but we can't use our own credit cards or IDs. Look I'm sure we can figure something out. Let's wait and see what Paul has to say."

CHAPTER 10

After checking with his XO, Captain McMurry went to his office, sent some emails and got caught up on his ships log. After a hot cup of coffee, he made some calls to one of his old navy buddies now working for military intelligence.

With every call he made, he got passed around from one bureaucrat to another. When he finally contacted his friend at the NSA, she said she couldn't talk on an open line. When he pressed her, she said she'd send him a message on his personal cell. While he waited, he contacted his old commander, Michael Goldsby, now a vice-admiral with the 6th fleet. Paul briefly explain the situation and, never one to back down from a challenge, the Vice Admiral agreed to help.

Admiral Goldsby, stationed at the Norfolk Naval base, was head of naval intelligence for the 6th fleet. He said he'd look into the case and he wanted to talk to them in person. He asked Captain McMurry to prep the helipad, he was sending a chopper right away to pick them up. Surprised by the Vice-Admirals sudden interest in their situation, went to give Polly the good news.

As he made his way through the hallway, and was on the stairs, he received a call on his personal cell phone. He picked up just as he was on his way top side, when he saw the caller ID was scrubbed, he thought it might be his friend Julie from the NSA. He always thought his friends in the intelligence community were a little too paranoid. He answered as he walked out on the foredeck and she said, "Hey Paul, just listen, I don't have any time for chit-chat. I'm out of the building on my lunch right now, but I did some digging and this thing we talked about, is buried deep. I don't have clearance, and from what I found. I don't think my bosses' boss could access the files. It's like super-duper "double-dog" top secret. Whatever your friends are into, I'd stay away, this is the kind of shit that gets people disappeared. Anyway, call me when you're in town, you owe me dinner," and she hung up.

Paul was understandably concerned following her warning. In addition to that, the fact that the Vice-Admiral, head of naval intelligence, would take such an immediate interest in their situation had his radar up. In a way, he was glad to be rid of the problem, but he was also concerned for Polly and her friend Tom. He couldn't help but wonder what she had gotten herself into. But in the end, he figured he had done all he could. With a navy helo on the way, soon they would be someone else's problem.

CHAPTER 11

Captain McMurry found Polly and Tom out on the fly bridge. Without giving too much away, he said, "Hey, I've got some good news. Polly you remember commander Goldsby? Well, he's a Vice Admiral now, head of naval intelligence. I briefed him on your situation, and he's agreed to help. In fact, he's sending a helo to pick you up and take you to his command center."

Polly, took Paul aside and said, "Did you find out anything about John, John Loveton, Tom's father?" Paul said, "Look Polly, everybody I talked to said the same thing. This is off limits. Highest security level. My friend at the NSA hinted that she could get fired for even talking to me. We're lucky we found a friend in Vice-Admiral Goldsby. He's always been a SOB, who loves to stick it to the top brass. When he was told it was "need to know only". I guess he just decided he needed to know, and the best way to do that was to pick you up instead of wading through the red tape."

Polly looked at Paul and said, "Goldsby was promoted to Vice-Admiral? Well bless my lucky stars! I always knew he was destined for a top spot. He was my CO at the Naval Academy."

"Well as soon as I mentioned your name he perked up. I guess he still has a soft spot for you," Paul said as he got on the radio and made sure his team was ready for an at-sea helo landing.

As Captain McMurry, left to tend to his duties, Polly turned to Tom and said, "Good news, we have found an unlikely ally. An old friend I can trust. I served under him at the academy. He's a Vice-Admiral now, that's like being a General in the army. He's got powerful friends and has agreed to help us. He is sending a helo to pick us up. Should be here within the hour. Let's see if we can get something to eat, I'm starved."

Tom just looked at her and said, "I'm feeling a little seasick, I don't know how you can eat at a time like this, I could use a cup of coffee though, please lead the way."

Polly found the chef preparing one of the many shift meals, and he had no trouble scrounging up some sandwiches for the two guests. As they sat, eating a surprisingly good lunch of grilled panini sandwiches, soup and home baked cookies, Polly said, "Our troubles for the near future should be over for now. Admiral Goldsby and I go back a long way. He's the one who encouraged me to join the special forces. As a logistics and operational analysts, I rose quickly through the ranks. He's tough as nails but a brilliant strategist."

Tom was still struggling to process recent events. For him, it was like living in a nightmare. He half expected to wake up in his cramped, 5th floor apartment in the city. He ate, in spite of his upset stomach, and wondered how all of this was going to end. He still wasn't any closer to finding his mom, and although Polly was resourceful and had gone above and beyond any expectations, he knew that finding Kate was now his top priority.

Just as Polly was finishing her last bite, a horn sounded from somewhere and Polly said, "That's got to be our ride. Let's go."

They both took their trays up to the dish counter, thanked the chef for a delicious lunch and made their way top side. Polly guided Tom towards the stern, where the crew has preparing for the approaching helicopter. As the ship turned into the wind, Captain McMurry appeared out of nowhere, had a few words with Polly and shaking Tom's hand wished him god's speed and was gone. One of the crew led Tom and Polly up a flight of stairs and onto the helo deck where the twin-engine Airbus Euro copter was just landing. They stayed out of the way until the chopper was secured and then were guided towards the cabin door where a surprisingly agile bear of a man, strapped them in and handed each one a helmet. Making sure they were secure, he closed the door and signaled to the pilot, and the sleek craft lifted off into the sky late afternoon sky.

Polly and Tom were taken to Norfolk as they were told, but to a Navy Intelligence ship off the coast, where Vice-Admiral Goldsby was waiting for them. The flight was uneventful and in 20 minutes they touched down on the deck of a large Navy ship.

Naval intelligence is one of the best kept secrets in the US military. The NSA and CIA are household names, but the earth is 3/4 ocean and Naval Intelligence covers all of it. With ships, submarines, aquatic drones and satellites, Naval intelligence was one of the premier intelligences gathering organizations in the world.

As they touched down, Tom gave Polly a questioning look, as if to say, "What the hell are we doing here?" As before, but in reverse, the flight officer helped Tom out of his safety harness and opened the door, where two of the flight crew were waiting to escort them to inside the massive ship intelligence gathering ship.

They were taken to a ready room where they were each given ID badges. Admiral Goldsby, was waiting for them in his office and as they entered, gave each one a handshake and had them sit at a table where they were each given a folder labeled "top secret" in bright red ink.

They were both speechless, and sensing the tension, the Admiral broke the silence. As he fingered the folder in front of him, he said, "Polly it's a great pleasure to see you again, I hear your doing valuable work with the marine animal research institute. And Mr. Loveton, may I call you Tom?" It was a rhetorical question and as Tom tried to answer, the admiral just continued talking. "Let me get right to the point," he said, as he leaned forward in his chair. Following my conversation with Captain McMurry, I did some checking. Seems like you got yourself in a bit of a mess, haven't you, he said looking directly at Tom."

Glancing at Polly, and then to the Admiral, Tom said, "Well sir, if you must know the truth, trouble has been following me the last couple of days like moss growing on the back of a hollow log."

"Yes, so I've heard," said the Admiral as he opened the folder in front of him. He said, "I had my staff work up this report. In it, you will find some very disturbing information regarding your father Dr. John Loveton. I suppose the news is good and bad in a way, depending on your perspective. From what I understand, your father disappeared about 20 years ago following a speech he gave at a UN conference on climate change. And as I understand it, his car crashed on the Pacific Coast highway just outside of Santa Monica. No body was discovered, and he was presumed drowned."

Tom nodded and said, "Yes, that's what I was told at the time."

"And only recently you've learned the truth. That he faked his death and fled the country. I can only imagine how you must be feeling at this point."

Not sure if he was asked a question, Tom remained silent.

The admiral's aide, who until then had gone unnoticed by either Tom or Polly, handed each of them a document. The admiral said, "Please sign at the bottom of the last page. This is a legal confidentiality disclosure form. Don't bother to try to read the fine print, we'll be here all day. It basically says, under penalty of death you will not disclose the contents of what you are about to learn to any person or persons etc....etc...."

A little shocked at the "under penalty of death reference," Polly and Tom found the pens that were neatly placed in front of them, both flipped to the last page, signed the documents and the aide promptly collected the papers and left the room.

Motioning for them to open the folders, the admiral said, "Inside the folders in front of you, is a detailed report of your father's activities since his disappearance almost 20 years ago. He was a controversial and brilliant man at the time and that hasn't changed."

"He went off the radar, following the crash and resurfaced several months later in New Zealand. Our intel community was able to track him through the funds he accessed through secret accounts scattered around the world. In the first 5 years following his disappearance, he went through an enormous amount of cash. Tom, did you know that at the time of your father faked his death, he was worth more than a billion dollars!"

"We have tried to penetrate his security with no luck. We sent a reconnaissance team to gather information on the nature of the facility and they never reported back."

In fact, all together we sent in three teams of our best people. The second one was captured by what they described as militarized robots. At first their version of events was met with extreme skepticism. Then one of our drones took these photos."

He opened a folder and laid several 8 by 10 black and white photos on the table. Each looked like stills taken from a science fiction movie. Dark figures wearing military like armor, hovering in the air like wasps, but without the wings, guarding a remote island off the coast of New Zealand.

"We have reason to believe that he has built a secret factory on an island off the northern coast of New Zealand. What he is building there we can only guess. He has the place guarded like Fort Knox. He even has his own private navy, complete with underwater drones disguised as sharks, guarding the waters around the island. If you open your folders to page 3, you can see satellite photos of the island. Tom what do you see?"

Looking down at the photo, and then at the admiral, Tom said, "It just looks like a big rock. I don't see evidence of a factory."

The admiral slammed his fist down on the table and said, "Precisely! It took years to figure out what he was doing. That island is a dormant basaltic dome volcano and he built his factory, right in the heart of it.

Now look at the next series of photos. These are pictures we obtained through a third party. The first one is a photo of inside the factory. Now, what were used to seeing, in a robotic factory, similar to the auto industry. Is a robotic assembly line manned by, well, men. Men and women to be more precise. But if you look carefully, this is a robotic factory, making robots by robots. This is so advanced; our top researchers can't even begin to figure out what is going on. When we first showed them these photos they laughed and said these had to be CGI. Yeah, I had to ask too. CGI means, computer generated image, like in the movies. The movie Terminator comes to mind when I see these pictures. This is light years ahead of anything in any industry, including dark money DARPA military projects."

Tom shifted in his seat and looking at Polly then back at the Admiral said, "Ok, so my dad faked his death, escaped to New Zealand, built a robotic factory making robots. What the hell does this have to do with me?"

"That's a good question," the Admiral said as he got up from his chair. He walked over to a large video screen and using a remote control, the Admiral turned on the screen which displayed a view of the earth from space. He said, "This is a view from one of our satellites, in the southern hemisphere. As we zoom in on New Zealand, we can see the island chain you father has claimed. It's called the Three Kings Island.

Geographically these islands formed separately from New Zealand. They are basaltic domes. And your father has taken advantage of that by building his secret factory inside the volcano. As you can see by the images, this is an extremely remote area. We have tried getting access to the island, but he is under the protection of the New Zealand government, which is in turn a British protectorate in name only."

Tom got up and said, "Thanks for the geography lesson admiral, I still don't see what any of this has to do with me, I haven't seen my dad since I was 10 years old. I don't think I could even pick him out of a line-up."

The admiral stared at Tom and he sat back in his chair like a house dog that just crapped on the carpet. As he paced the floor in the now cramped office, the admiral said. "The men that kidnapped your students were actually after you. And the men that killed the caretakers at your mother's estate, were after her. Our government is not the only organization interested in your father's work. There's billions of dollars at stake here and more important than that, some of the predictions your father made regarding the imminent danger of climate change are starting to come true.

The admiral turned to face the screen and the image changed to the view of the northern hemisphere. He said, "These images were taken recently from a weather satellite over the north pole. As you can see, all of the ice that usually covers this region is gone. The same is true for Greenland, and the south pole isn't faring any better."

The screen now changed from image to image, all over the world, areas that were once covered in snow and ice year-round were now barren rock or open water. The admiral, turned off the screen and sat down at the table again and said, "I won't bore you with the details, but things are getting serious."

Tom looked at the admiral and said, "Again, I am well aware of the dangers of climate change. But I'll ask again, what does any of this have to do with me?"

"Tom, I believe that you and your mom are targets for those that would like to use you to get to your father. And I have reason to believe that there are secret forces within our government that may have some involvement in recent events."

Silent until now, Polly spoke up and said," So are you saying that members of our government tried to kill us this morning?"

Putting up his hand, the Admiral said, "Polly, as you know there are "black ops" elements in our government that operate outside the law. No, I don't think they were trying to kill you, I think they were just trying to disable your boat, so they could capture Tom. Apparently, they weren't prepared for your escape from your father's estate, and their plan B didn't go so well."

Getting angry now Polly said, "What about the caretakers, what were they, collateral damage too?"

Trying his best to sound calm, the admiral said, "According to my classified briefing, the men had instructions to safely take Kate into custody, they didn't count on her attack dogs and two military trained caretakers. Apparently, things flew out of control rather quickly when the dogs attacked, and the men overreacted when the caretakers intervened.

The men who kidnapped the kids were mercenaries who were after Tom. Our team moved in to get your mother when we intercepted some of their communications. Fortunately, you rescued the kids, or who knows what would have happened."

"Polly, from what I've learned, two of the men at your father's estate, were FBI and the other two were military contractors. The FBI had instructions to take Tom into custody. We're not sure about the mission of other team, but it's obvious things got out of control when Tom escaped. Two of the contractors were killed in the helicopter crash."

Dumbfounded by the level of stupidity being explained, Tom said, "So let me see if I've got this straight. You have been monitoring both my mother and me, maybe for years. Then all of a sudden, you have intel that a nefarious group which remains a mystery, was on their way to kidnap me and my mother Kate. So, you sent in a team to get her and ended up killing two innocent people. Meanwhile, my mother escaped, and no one knows where she ended up. Then the men that were after me, kidnapped my class to black mail me into doing who knows what. After Polly rescued the kids, our government sent in a team to capture me against my will. They fail and with Polly's help I escape. They chase us in a helicopter and start shooting at us at sea. Polly disabled their chopper and two more people are killed. Is that about, right?"

Admiral Goldsby looked sheepishly at Tom and Polly and said, "Well, when you put it that way it sounds pretty bad doesn't it?"

Tom, looking hard at the admiral said, "Did anyone think that maybe if you just came to me and asked for my help, we could have avoided all this mess?"

"Well frankly no. In the fog of war, battlefield decisions don't always go as planned. When the intel came through that a team was in route to pick you up, they assumed that your mother was in danger as well. I am truly sorry for the loss of your friends. However, regarding your mother Kate. We may have a lead on where she might be."

Tom said, "Wait a minute. You are just telling me this now. Talk about burying the lead. Where the hell is, she? I've been worried sick."

The Admiral just looked at Tom and said, "Yes I'm sorry, but listen here Tom, this is what we know. Normal radar would not pick up a low flying ultralight. But we run regular AWAC flights up and down the coast 24/7 looking for drug smugglers. Going back over the tapes from that day. It looks like a small craft, took off from Nantucket Island, flew up the coast and landed somewhere in upper New York State. We can't be exactly sure of the landing area; their coverage only extends so far inland."

With growing frustration Tom said, "You're only telling me this now?

"As I said, in the fog of war...we can't know all the facts in real time."

Angry now Tom said, "Don't give me that fog of war bullshit. How long have you known about this?"

"Again, I'm sorry. When dealing with multiple government agencies, information is often a casualty. We just analyzed the AWAC tapes while you were on your way here. Listen son, I only just found out about this cluster fuck a couple of hours ago. I'm trying to do what I can to protect you, but there are powerful forces at work here."

"Ok, I get it. Best laid plans of mice and men and all that. I think I may know where Kate is. My family has a farm in upper NY state and now I'm sure that's where she landed. We were just talking about going there to hide out for a while. But we weren't sure how to get there."

"Well, I can help with that. We would also like to talk to your mother. According to this brief, the NSA has been monitoring her for years. Apparently, she has been communicating with your father ever since his disappearance. We are hoping that she can shed some light on his activities over the last few years."

"Why the hell is everybody so concerned with my father's activities. What's he building, a nuclear bomb or something?"

"Here's what I can tell you. Again, this is top secret. The New Zealand government recently announced their intention to launch an orbital spacecraft. You're probably wondering why this is significant? New Zealand has never had a "Space Program." So obviously our government agencies that monitor these things were understandably concerned. After some interagency cooperation, it was revealed that it is your father's company, "LRC" is actually doing the launch; in cooperation with the New Zealand government of course."

The Admiral opened another folder marked top secret and laid out several more photos on the table. He said to Tom, "See this area here," as he pointed to an area marked in red marker. "We believe that this is a launch pad that your father has constructed to put satellites into space. For what purpose, we don't know."

Trying his best to sound calm, Tom said, "Ok, now that all the facts have been established, what do we do now? I've got a class to teach."

"As part of a wider investigation into your father's factory, we'd like to ask for your cooperation."

"Well you could have asked me for that a long time ago and saved everybody a lot of trouble."

"Yes, well, like I said, I only just found out about this today. That's why I scooped the two of you up. I want to get to the bottom of what's going on just as much as you do. I'm afraid that too many of those in positions of power in our government shoot first and ask questions later. Let's start with getting you to a safe place. If Kate is already there, the family farm seems like a good place to start. We can fly you in and have a security detail for your protection. Do you have an address or phone number? We need to do a recon, prior to your arrival."

"No, actually I don't. I haven't been there myself in years. I could probably find it on a map."

"Ok, that'll work. I'll have you work with my logistics coordinator to locate the farm. By the way, have you tried contacting your mother, since her disappearance?"

"No, I haven't had time. Besides, I left my cell phone back in my classroom. All my numbers are in there."

"We got her number through her carrier and she either has her phone off or there is no signal out at the farm, if that's where she is."

"I'm going to have an officer escort you to the lounge where you can get some rest. I'll work out the logistics at the farm and try to get a hold of your mother."

As they were escorted to the officer's lounge, Tom was starting to feel somewhat better. Confident that he found out what happened to his mother was like a weight lifted from his shoulders. As Tom sat down in one of the uncomfortable plastic sofas, Polly poured them each a cup of stale coffee. She came over and tried to soothe Tom's condition.

As he took the coffee he said, "Hey thanks, you know Polly, it makes sense that she would go to the farm. I never imagined that the tiny ultralight, could make it all the way to Up-State NY without refueling. I'll feel a lot better if I could talk to her. I need answers, I just don't even know what questions to ask. How do I start? Um, gee mom, I just heard that dad faked his death and is really alive. And, all these years, you never told me anything. How's that conversation supposed to go?"

Polly looked at Tom with tears in her eyes said," Tom, I know how hard this must be for you, she must have had a good reason to keep all this a secret. Look at the upside. Your dad is alive and well in living in New Zealand. And it sounds like he's been doing some very important work."

Tom set his coffee down and sitting back on the sofa said, "Polly, I don't know what to feel or think. So far, four people are dead, my students were kidnapped, my mom had to escape Nantucket Island in an ultralight, I'm told that my dad is launching a rocket into outer space from a secret island factory. I don't know how anything good can come out of this."

Just then, an officer entered the room and said, "Mr. Loveton, Ms. Johnson, Admiral Goldsby would like to see you now. Please come with me."

Tom, still hobbling on his sprained ankle, followed behind Polly as they walked down the narrow hallway to the Admirals office.

The admiral was sitting behind his desk and as they entered, he rose from his seat and motioned for them to sit on the red leather sofa as he sat to their right in a matching wingback armchair.

Looking sternly at Tom, he said, "Listen here son, I know you've been through a lot. You didn't ask for any of this, but there comes a time in a man's life when he is asked by his country to step up. I'm afraid that this is your time. Your country needs you."

"Leaning forward and looking the admiral in the eye, Tom said, "What can I do? I'm just a high school teacher. Polly is the one who rescued the kids and helped me escape. I'm no James Bond."

The Admiral smiled at Tom's Bond reference and said, "We will have our people with you every step of the way. I know this won't be easy for you. But what we need you to do, is make contact with your dad. Try to gain his trust, get into the factory and report back to us on what's going on."

Looking at Polly and then at the Admiral, Tom said, "So you want me to spy on my own father? The man who faked his death and fled the country. What if he doesn't let me in?"

"We feel that once he learns of the danger his family is in, he will want you close."

"How am I supposed to get to an island guarded by robotic sharks?"

"Well, we were thinking it would be better if he didn't know you were working for us. We can have you and Polly attached to a US State Department diplomatic team in New Zealand. Once we have you in position, we will reach out to our connections in the New Zealand government and see what happens. We feel that once he learns that you are part of the diplomatic team, he will let you in.

So that's our plan in a nutshell. We will brief you on the details later. I know you must be tired. I will have a steward show you to your quarters. I'm sure after a hot meal and a good night's rest, you'll feel better in the morning."

The Admiral got up and as he said, Tom and Polly were shown to their sparse quarters. After a shower and a nap, Tom woke and realized he hadn't eaten is what seemed like days. There was a soft rap on his door and Polly entered the shadow filled room. She quietly spoke, "Tom, are you awake?"

"Yeah, come in, I just woke," he said as she slid in the cramped single bed. "You get any sleep?

He said as he yawned. "Yeah, a little. I couldn't get the image of the crash out of my head. What a cluster-fuck. I'm starving," Tom said as he held her in his arms.

"Yeah me too," Polly said as she yawned.

"Think we can rustle up some grub from the mess hall, or whatever you call it."

"Yeah, they are always serving on a ship like this. They run a 24/7 operation, and someone is always starting a shift or ending one. I just don't know where the cafeteria is on the floating city. Just then a phone rang from somewhere. Polly jumped out of bed at the sound and turned on the small desk lamp attached to the wall, just near the bed.

"Hello?" She said with a sleepy rasp to her voice.

It was one of the crew assigned to their quarters. The admiral apparently assigned a steward to their quarters and she was instructed to meet their every need.

"The is midshipman Carol Stockton, I was instructed to check on you and when I got no response when I called your cabin, I assumed you would be with Mr. Loveton. I have a cart of food prepared for you if you're hungry."

"Oh yes, that would be great, just give us a few minutes to get dressed," Polly said nudging Tom who had dozed off again and was silently snoring. She hung up the phone and turned on the overly bright overhead light. Tom groaned and said, "Any chance they have room service on this barge?"

"Yes, as a matter of fact, a food cart is on its way. So, get up and get dressed, I'll be right back," she said as she went to her room to get the robe the steward had left out for her."

After a delicious late-night snack of grilled panini sandwiches and cream of tomato soup, they drifted off to sleep on the cramped single bed.

The admiral gave instructions to let them sleep in, as he prepared for their departure. After the inter-agency mess, was explained to the pentagon, they were happy to hand off the whole cluster fuck to Vice Admiral Goldsby. He arranged to have Tom and Polly flown out to the farm via Navy chopper with a strong security detail. He was taking no chances and oversaw the planning himself.

CHAPTER 12

Kate woke up early on a bright and clear September morning. Feeling restless, she went out for a quick two-mile run. When she returned, she found the front door wide open. An alarm bell went off in her head, she lived alone and had two caretakers that lived on the island year-round.

She was sure she had shut the front door on her way out for her morning run. Her live-in caretakers, Dale and Buffy were former Navy officers and had worked as research assistants for her husband John at Stanford before he disappeared. They lived in a cottage adjacent to the main house and they rarely came over uninvited unless there was some kind of emergency.

The early morning sun was shining through the swaying willow trees as Kate entered the half-open front door of the two-story Cape Cod style home. Kate sensed something was wrong, and her suspicions were confirmed as she entered the living room and saw the door to John's study was ajar. As she peered past the partially open door and entered the shuttered wood paneled study. She gasped as she took in the mess. Bookshelves were up-ended, pictures were torn off the wall, desk drawers were emptied on the floor and John's old Apple PC was smashed in pieces on the desk.

Her thoughts immediately went to Dale and Buffy. If there was a break-in, being x-military, she knew they could handle themselves. Maybe that's why John hired them in the first place. She was never sure. There was really no reason to have two such obviously overqualified former military officers as live-in caretakers; yet they seemed happy. Buffy was an artist and Dale a writer, and they both enjoyed the quiet solitude of the island and Kate thought nothing of their occasional trips to far off places.

The morning sun was just clearing the eastern ridge and the bright sunlight shone through the shadows on the north lawn as she gazed out the large bay window. She picked up the phone with a direct extension to the cottage but found the line dead. She crossed the living room and passed the kitchen as she made her way out the sliding glass doors on to the deck. The ocean was calm as a light breeze grazed her cheek and white puffy clouds filled the horizon. She gazed out over the back lawn and called for the dogs as she watched a large schooner pushed by a stiff ocean breeze across Nantucket Sound. Her tracks followed behind her as she stepped through the wet grass, still damp from the night's rain. She thought it odd that a track of grass had been matted down heading towards the boat house. But it was time to start winterizing and the boat house was used more for storage than anything else, so she thought little of it.

As she approached the small cottage, she noticed the back-porch door was left open and she called again for the dogs to heal, but they were nowhere in sight. She continued across the lawn, quickening her pace as she went. Growing more concerned, she called out for the dogs again, she was surprised they were not out in the backyard laying in the morning sun or playing with their favorite chew toys.

She called out to Dale and Buffy as she climbed the steps to the screened-in porch. Now, worried about where the dogs had gotten off too, she knocked on the open cottage door and said, "Dale, Buffy, is anyone home?" She walked through the porch and into the living room and was horrified by what she saw. It looked like a mini tornado had gone through the house. Lamps, tables and chairs were smashed and strewn across the room. She called out again but was only met with the rapid beat of her own heart, and as she scanned the small living room, she saw the bodies of her German Shepherds, Thor and Zeus, lying on a throw rug covered in blood.

She slipped as she crossed the polished wood floor and realized it was covered in streaks of fresh blood. Horrified, she ran to the kitchen where she saw Dale and Buffy lying awkwardly on the floor, small pools of blood surrounding their bodies.

She ran to the living room where she tried the phone, but just as in the main house, the line was dead. Panic-stricken, she instinctively ran out the back door and up to the main house where she ran upstairs to her bedroom. She grabbed a small pre-packed backpack, hidden deep in the recesses of her closet. Still wearing her running suit, she gathered a few things from the master bathroom, and stuffed them into her pack as she ran downstairs.

She grabbed her cell phone and purse, and left out the back door, running towards the western edge of the estate where she kept an ultra-lite in an old tobacco barn. As she reached the barn, she used her cell phone to call and warn Tom. All this time, she had wanted desperately to tell Tom the truth about his father. She got through as she opened the barn doors, and tried to warn Tom of the attack, but when he answered he said that he was busy and would call her back. She called back several times, but the calls went unanswered.

She threw her pack into the open-air cockpit as she did a pre-flight inspection. She then topped off the extended range fuel tanks from an antique gravity fed pump system. Never thinking she'd ever need it; she kept the small customized plane flight ready at all times. She started the custom build turbo charged engine, slowly moving the plane through the barn doors and out into the clearing, where a makeshift runway was cut into the grassy meadow. Still reeling from the images running through her mind from the cottage, with shaking hands she pushed the throttle forward as the small plane quickly lifted off the ground and into the bright summer sun.

With tears streaming down her face, she thought back to just how she ended up fleeing for her life in an ultra-light flying up the east coast.

After faking his death and fleeing to Mexico. John & Kate had kept in touch through the fledgling internet. Back then, a loosely connected system of 14k modems communicating over phone lines, was used mostly by scientists sharing data across the world. It was no different for Kate and John, as he relied on her technical expertise to make the breakthroughs that he needed to fulfill his dream of building advanced robots capable of working in the zero-gravity environment of space. She knew about the underground factory he built on an island off the north shore of New Zealand and had helped with the advances he had made in science and technology. However, she refused to heed his warnings and insisted on living the carefree life a retired college professor.

What she didn't know, and what John suspected, was that their communications, had been constantly monitored, ever since his disappearance nearly 20 years before. The NSA had increased their interest in John's business in the last few years, as the advances made in John's secret robotic factory were of major interest to the US military. They suspected that John was selling secrets to the Chinese government, in violation of US trade laws. But with John's factory outside US jurisdiction, there was little they could do other than monitor the heavily encrypted communication coming from the factory.

John was secretly sharing information with several Chinese scientists. One of his main concerns was that the devastation to the Earth's ecosystem was spinning out of control faster than he predicted. He knew that he alone, would not be able to save enough of the human race to maintain the ethnic diversity needed to populate the habispheres that he envisioned would one day save the human race from virtual extinction.

John was very close to launching his first satellite containing an automated industrial 3D printer, designed to begin the construction of the world's first habisphere. His first of its kind, reusable space delivery system, used a combination of advanced chemical booster rockets and a next generation second stage solar sail technology.

Kate was feeling the fatigue following the adrenaline surge she experienced while escaping the island. She was flying low over the Atlantic on a pre-arranged flight plan in the event of an emergency. She booted up the iPad fixed to the control panel and brought up the mapping program. The GPS marker showed her location on the map showing the pre-selected route to their farmhouse in upper New York State just south of Albany.

With the extended fuel tanks and turbo charged engine, traveling at 150 mph, given the cross winds she estimated the flight would take 45 minutes to an hour. The trouble was, Kate had no chance to warn the elderly couple living on the 250-acre farm that she was on her way. She'd only made the flight once before at John's insistence and there was no way to be sure the dirt lane in the back 40, would be cleared for her arrival. It was close to harvest time, and she knew there was chance the lane would be blocked by one piece of farm equipment or another.

The original 8-bedroom farmhouse was built in the 1700s and was still a working farm, growing a mix of corn, soybeans, alfalfa and some livestock. As Kate approached the farm from the east, she buzzed the main house, hoping to attract the attention of someone on the ground. Olive and Ellery had lived on the farm since they moved from New York City following their retirement. Olive was at the local farmers market, where she sold fresh eggs, and strawberries, while Ell, was out getting work done on his old truck.

She didn't see anyone on the ground near the house, so she turned North and headed towards the back 40, where she saw some farm hands tending the sheep. Not wanting to run the risk of scaring the livestock, she circled back to the main house to survey the driveway for a landing. She estimated that if she flew low over the barn, she could make it under the power line and onto the gravel driveway with room to spare. Turning east over the pond, she circled back and flew low over the barn.

She landed safely on the gravel driveway, made a U-turn and guided the small plane towards one of the outbuildings. She powered down, grabbed her bag, and checked her cell phone connection. One of the things she loved about the untouched beauty of Northern New York state, was the backwoods country charm and lack of technology. Today she cursed under her breath when she realized, she had no cell reception and no wireless internet. She walked towards the main house; the long low front porch reminded her of the main street scenes in the old westerns she was so fond of. As she reached out to turn the small brass knob of the bell on the intricately carved wooden door, she watched as a small mouse as it scurried across the old wooden floor of the original farmhouse porch. She found the door half-open and called out as she entered, "Anyone home? It's Kate."

She entered the small farmhouse kitchen, and marveled at the pristine condition the old couple kept the place in. For her it was like walking into a time machine every time she came for a visit, which she tried to do at least once a year. The original wood burning stove was still in regular use and was warming the room from the chill of the nighttime mountain air.

There was a small ceramic pot of coffee on the warm side of the stove and she got a mug from a shelf and helped herself to a cup. Just then Ell came through the porch door and having seen the small plane parked out back, surmised that Kate was in for a surprise visit. Ell was a big man, even in his twilight years.

He stood a good 6'3" and tipped the scales at around 400 lbs. As he reached out to greet her, he said in a loud baritone voice, "Kate how wonderful to see you, Olive is at the market and should be home soon, you should have called ahead, we weren't expecting you till next month."

Kate always planned a visit during the fall seasonal color change. She said something about painters and that a storm had knocked out her landline as she sipped her coffee and looked out the back window at squirrel, busily storing nuts for the winter. El said, "Well, whatever the reason, we're glad for the company, your room is just as you left it last year. Olive will make up the bed and I'll bring up some fresh firewood, the nights are starting to get chilly this time of year."

It was close to lunchtime and never one to miss a meal, El looked out the window expecting to see Olive returning from the market at any minute. She had promised fried chicken for lunch and knowing that she always made extra for his late-night snacks, he knew there would be plenty for Kate as well. He walked towards the stove, and as he restocked the wood burner said, "The harvest is going to be a good one this year. We had an early spring, adding to our short growing season. We had a little blight on the beans this summer due to the heavy rains, but all in all we're ahead of last year." Ell was an accountant by trade, a former Wall Street executive. He was good with a hammer and tools, but never having farmed his whole life, he left the actual work to local farm hands. Yet he was a well-respected manager and treating the staff like family.

Kate just listened politely as he filled her in on the doings of the farm. Her mind was miles away, and she said something about using the phone as she went into the tack room and sat at the large picture window overlooking the large vegetable garden Olive always planted every spring.

She picked up the rotary style princess phone from the side table and was about to make a call when she realized, she didn't know who to call. She couldn't call John, not on a regular phone. She wanted to call the Nantucket police but didn't want them to trace the call to the farm. She was trying to remember the code to block the caller ID, when she heard Olive bringing in groceries from the market. She heard whispering and assumed El was filling Olive in on her unexpected arrival. She stood and as she approached the kitchen, Olive came into the room with a bunch of flowers and said, "Oh Katie my dear, how wonderful to see you. You should have called ahead, but no matter, here you are. Is everything alright, you seem out of sorts dear."

Olive put the flowers in a vase on a table by the window and as she reached out to give Kate a hug said, "Lunch will be ready in ready in about 20 minutes, why don't you go upstairs and lie down for a bit you look tired."

Kate, not knowing what else to do, said, "Yes, I am feeling a bit peckish after my flight. Maybe I'll do that, just call me when lunch is ready," and she made her way up the rickety staircase to her room.

Kate woke from a quick nap, to the delicious aroma of fried chicken. She was in such a deep sleep at first, she couldn't remember where she was. Then the horrible images of the caretaker cottage flooded her mind and she started to cry. She got up from the four-post canopy bed and went to the window. Trying desperately to wipe the images from her mind she thought back to when she was a little girl, playing with her cousins on the back lawn of the farm, horseback riding through the fields and picking fresh vegetables from the garden.

She wiped tears from her eyes as she turned to go downstairs. It wasn't time for grieving yet. Her mother's premonition told her that Tom was in danger and that somehow, she had to warn him.

CHAPTER 13

Admiral Goldsby's attempts to reach the farmhouse over a landline proved unsuccessful. Apparently, the couple caring for the old farmstead, changed the number after Kates local attorney passed away and stopped paying the bill. Tom couldn't remember their last name and the local phone company had switched to an automated call center system. Even with the world's largest investigative team at his disposal, no one in Naval Intelligence could get a call through to the farm.

The Local FBI reached out to the local Sheriff's office and without revealing too much, asked that a squad of Sheriff's deputies be dispatched to the farm and wait for instructions.

Of course, as with all small-town agencies, the request for assistance from the FBI was taken out of context, and the county SWAT team was dispatched, along with almost every available squad car in the area.

El was just getting ready to put burgers and fresh sweet corn on the grill for the crew's afternoon meal, when an army of local law enforcement officers descended on the property. He was first alerted by the sound of a police helicopter flying overhead. Then he heard the sound of several cars on the gravel driveway.

With a platter of burgers in his hands, El watched as five police cars and a SWAT team vehicle parked on the back lawn.

Olive was watching out the kitchen window as a line of police cars descended on the property, when the phone rang. She answered the wall phone while trying to balance a tray full of corn with one hand and answer the phone with the other. It was the Sheriff's office. "Hello," she said warily as she watched a Sheriff's deputy approach El out at the grill.

"Hello, this is the sheriff's office, is that you Olive?"

"Yes, how can I help you?"

"This is Deputy sheriff, Louise Mitchell, you remember me from that time down to the farmer's market when those kids tried to steal your bushel of strawberries?"

Laughing at the thought, and holding the phone on her shoulder while still trying to balance the overloaded platter of sweet corn she said, "Yes I remember, what's all this about? There's a deputy out on the lawn, and a helicopter about to land on my rutabagas."

"Well Olive, that's why I'm calling. We had a hard time tracking down your new number."

"Ok, you found it. Now can you tell me what in the dickens is going on?"

"We're trying to find Kate. Kate Loveton, she wouldn't happen to be there would she."

"Yes, she got here yesterday. Should I put her on?"

"No, it's too late for that. Our people will talk to her, I guess I was just trying to warn you before everyone got there but I'm a little late."

"Ok, I'm right in the middle of cooking supper for the crew so if you don't mind."

"Oh yes of course dear, sorry to bother you, have a nice day," and she hung up. Somewhat startled at the call, and commotion out on the lawn, Olive put the tray of corn on the table and worried for Kate, turned to go upstairs to her room. As she turned, Kate was there in the kitchen door frame. Olive said, "There was a call for you dear. It was the sheriff. I don't know why they're calling but after I told them you were here, they hung up."

Looking out the kitchen window, Kate said, "I should have expected they'd find me here. I'm sorry Olive, I didn't say anything before, but there was some trouble back at the island."

"I knew something was amiss. Whatever it is honey we'll always be here for you, you know that," Olive said as she handed Kate a cup of tea. "Now tell me dear what happened."

"No, I can't. I mean not now," Kate said as she sipped her tea.

Just then there was a knock on the screen door and a sheriff deputy poked her head through the door and said, "Olive, my I come in?"

Olive looked at her and said, "You're halfway there already, you might as well come in. Looks like you brought some friends." Trying to sound welcoming she said, "You want some coffee dear?"

Sheriff Weatherspoon stepped through the door frame and seeing that Olive wasn't alone said, "You must be Kate, we've been looking for you."

Leaning against the kitchen table and sipping her tea, she said, "Well It looks like you found me. What do you want? The whole lot of you are trespassing. I'd call my lawyer if I had her number."

"There's no need to get in a huff. We were sent here by the FBI. Seems they need to talk to you bout sumptn mighty impotant."

"That figures," she said as she wavered a little suddenly feeling lightheaded.

The phone rang again and slightly exasperated, Olive answered, "Hello".

It was Tom calling from sea. "Hi Olive, it's been years, how's El?"

Growing impatient with all the confusion, she said, "I'm in the middle of making supper. Your Moms here let me put her on."

She said, "Here Kate, excuse me," as she handed her the phone, picked up the platter of corn and went outside to help Ell with the cooking.

Kate said, "Hello Tom, is it really you? I was so worried."

"Yes, mom it's me. Are you safe?"

"Of course, I'm safe, there's an army of police parked out on the lawn."

"We are on our way there, I mean I'm on the way. I mean well, it's complicated. I'm just relieved to hear your voice, after what happened at the island, I thought the worst."

"Oh Tom, you know? How? I mean, of course. I suppose someone was bound to find the bodies. And once they couldn't me find I guess; oh, Tom it was so horrible."

"Yes mom, I was there. I was at the house; I saw what happened. There's more. But I can't talk now. Like I said, I'm on my way."

"What's going on Tom? Where are you? Are you safe?"

"Yes mom, like I said, I'll be there soon. We have a lot to talk about."

"Yes, I know dear, I have so much to tell you."

"I'll be there soon." And with that the line went dead.

CHAPTER 14

The SWAT team created a perimeter around the main house, while the sheriff's deputies were scattered around the farm fields. The regional FBI office sent in a team to coordinate logistics and provide a personal security detail for Kate.

Tom and Polly arrived via Navy chopper with a Seal Team 6, for security. Trailers were brought in to house the force assigned to the security detail.

Kate was debriefed by the FBI, while Tom and Polly settled into separate rooms on the second floor. Tom was still in shock from the events of the last two days and was in no shape to face his mother. Learning the truth about his father, along with everything else was just too much for him to handle.

Polly softly rapped on his bedroom door and slowly entered the dimly lit room. The sun was just setting over the mountains casting long shadows across the wood floor.

A slight chill was in the air, and Polly moved toward the open window. Tom, lying on top of the bedspread, got up, and as Polly closed the window, she turned to face him and said, "How are you feeling?"

He reached out to her and they embraced. For the first time since finding the Jones at Nana's, he let himself relax. A tear rolled down his cheek and Polly held him tightly guiding him towards the bed.

Kate was standing at the door, and her heart sank as she realized it was time for Tom to know the truth. A truth she had hoped she'd never have to tell. Polly looked up, and seeing Kate, nervously got off the bed and said, "I'll leave you two alone." Kate entered the room and sat on the antique couch along the wall facing the bed. Tom looked up and pushing himself off the bed sat awkwardly on the side chair facing the door.

Not knowing what to say, he just leaned forward staring at the floor. Kate was the first to speak as she moved closer to where Tom was sitting. She reached out and holding Tom's hand said, "I'm so sorry dear for everything. I wanted to tell you about your father so many times, but I just couldn't. He needed to disappear. It was the only way he could continue his work. How much have they told you?"

"Not much, he said through tears."

Tom, I am so sorry, I couldn›t tell you about what really happened, but it was for his safety and yours. There are some very bad, very powerful people who were after your father. And that›s the reason he faked his death and went into hiding. He was afraid they would stop at nothing to silence him, and he feared for his life and yours. I have been working with your father to create new technologies at his factory and that›s about all I can tell you right now.

"I still can't believe half of what they're saying." And looking up for the first time he said, "Is it true mom? The things they're saying, it seems like a nightmare. Have you seen or talked to him?"

She hesitantly, looked at Tom and said, "Yes, I have a Sat phone we use for secure communications. We don't talk as much as we used to. He's very busy trying to save humanity."

"But at what cost mom, I mean we were a family. Taking a father from a son so young...it's just hard to understand. After all this time, what am I supposed to think?"

"Your father has always regretted what happened... the way he left. He was desperate and heartbroken. I know it's hard to understand his motives. But he did it for us. I mean for humanity."

"Ok I get it mom. What are we supposed to do now? They want me to spy on him. Why can't he just come out of hiding. What's really going on? They're talking like he's some kind of mad scientist or something."

"I can only imagine what you're going through. Scientist yes, mad I don't know. Only time will tell. What I can tell you is that your father still loves you deeply, and now he's going to want to see you. At least give him a chance. He's been through so much. He was badly injured in a lab accident. They put him back together, but he's changed. I mean it changed him. For better or worse I don't know. You'll have to decide for yourself."

"What do you mean changed? What happened to him?"

He lost both legs and an arm. He was fitted with advanced prosthetics. He's recovered, but somehow different. I can't explain. His focus has shifted. But he's still your father. Look Tom, I know you've been through a lot, a good night's sleep will help bring everything into better focus."

CHAPTER 15

After a fit-full night sleep, Tom woke following a nightmare where he was being chased by an unseen creature, like a rat in a maze running this way and that until he came to a clearing with a harvest moon just above a mountainous tree line. Lost in the wilderness, he heard the sound of baying hounds, running wildly he came upon a high grassy hill. He climbed the hill being chased by gigantic hounds biting at his heels. He would advance a little then slowly slide down towards the ferocious animals. This scenario was repeated over and over again until he woke in a cold sweat. Looking around the room it took a moment for him to remember where he was.

Polly was at his bedside. He opened his eyes and seeing Polly slowly rocking back and forth he realized he was safe at the farm. He thought, if not for his old friend Polly, he probably be in jail or worse.

Still in her night clothes, Polly said "Good morning sleepy head," as she rose and stretched. I thought you were going to sleep all day. It's already late you silly goose. We have to get moving. The Admiral will be here soon. Apparently, they have some big plans for you, so rise and shine," she said as she made her way towards the door.

Tom was having a late breakfast out on the front porch as he warily watched the Admiral's chopper land in the backyard and was a bit annoyed at the intrusion. The Admiral arrived in a Navy helo with a contingent of aids and wanted to meet with Kate, Tom and Polly right away.

With Olives assistance they set up in the dining room, and then she and Ellery were escorted to a waiting SUV. The Admiral wanted no leaks and that meant that the only people allowed in the house during their meeting were on a "need to know" basis only.

Still in a bathrobe Tom quickly finished his food and followed the parade of aids into the old farmhouse. Tom went upstairs to get dressed while the dining room was checked for listening devices. He came downstairs and was surprised to see everyone already seated. Feeling a bit like he was late for his own party, Tom sat at the only vacant chair, situated between Polly and his mom and facing the Admiral. The admiral started by saying, "I want to thank you all for your cooperation. I know this must be a difficult time for you and my apologies for the intrusion."

Shuffling some papers and whispering to an aid standing at his side he looked around the table and said, "Things have changed significantly since we last spoke. There's been an incident at Kings Island. The scheduled launch of you father's first satellite was early this morning."

We don't have actual eyes in space, however, observations from ground-based telescopes indicate that the launch device is some kind of robotic 3D printer. And that this device, which by the way, is light years ahead of anything we know of. Is constructing some kind of platform, or space station? We're not really sure."

"Here are some photos we obtained from our partners at the NSA. As you can see. There appears to be some kind of robotic drone assisting the construction."

"As far as we know, no laws were violated by this launch. New Zealand is claiming this is part of their space program and like any other nation, have the right to put objects in orbit like any other country."

"They did notify the UN that they were in the process of building a rocket launch system and that a launch was imminent. At the time we didn't take them seriously for obvious reasons."

"There is another development. Now I'm no scientist, but I'm told by our scientific community that this was no ordinary launch. This was the first use of a carbon fiber nanotube solar sail. And that if perfected, means that they have the capability to launch vehicles into earth orbit faster and more efficiently than ever before. Another thing I'm told, is that the launch vehicle was like something out of a sci-fi movie. It launched like a rocket, deployed the solar sail in the outer atmosphere, released the satellite, then using the solar sail as a break, flew like a plane back to earth. They estimate the turnaround for this type of craft would be about two or three days. That means that they could launch six to ten vehicles a month, maybe more."

Now looking directly at Kate, he said, "How much of what we are seeing here were you aware of."

Kate shifted nervously in her seat, and clearing her now parched throat said, "Um, well, I was part of the initial design team that built a lot of the islands infrastructure. I have advanced degrees in structural and electrical engineering. But this was not anything I was part of. John and his team have made some incredible advances in technology in the last few years. But this is beyond anything that I was aware of. In fact, John and I haven't had any communication for several months."

"Ok. Well there are some other recent developments we need to cover. Tom, it seems that your father has been working with the Chinese government as a source of raw materials for his factory in exchange for what we believe is advanced technical information. Now for an ordinary citizen or US corporation, this would be a violation of international law. But for starters, he is supposed to be dead, and until we can apprehend him and prove beyond a reasonable doubt that he is alive, we cannot initiate a case for his extradition. In addition, your father is wanted on several very serious charges. He is still a US citizen and therefore subject to US espionage and tax laws. But seriously, we really just want to talk to him. He could help advance our technical capabilities tremendously."

"On another front, several of your father's earlier predictions on climate change are starting to come true. I truly believe that his message would be well received at this point in time. Tom, I'm asking on behalf of a grateful nation, will you help us?"

Tom looked at the Admiral, and then around the table. He shifted in his seat and said, "Where was the government 20 years ago when my father needed it the most. He was threatened, attacked and ridiculed; his work sabotaged. I've read the reports and newspaper articles. I lost my father 20 years ago because a nation and a world he was trying to protect, turned its back on him. Now you want my help. Why should I trust you? Look at what happened at Nana's. Four people were killed because of your carelessness."

Taken offence at the insinuation, Admiral Goldsby said, "Look here Tom, you know those at this table had nothing to do with any of that."

"What's the difference. You. Them. Whoever. You're all part of the same fucked up system that is killing the planet. I can't blame my dad for faking his death and going into hiding. I would have probably done the same thing."

"Well, said the Admiral, "The apple doesn't far from the tree does it?"

Getting angry Tom said, "What the hell is that supposed to mean? Do you want my help or not?"

"I'm sorry son, we are all under a lot of stress. Why don't we take a break? I think I smell roast chicken cooked up by my personal chef, we can have a meal and then talk about your future."

Tom, Polly and Kate ate lunch out on the back patio; far from the prying eyes and ears of their uninvited guests. Kate was the first to speak. "He has a point Tom. If your father is sharing secrets with the Chinese, it could be a violation of international law."

"Mom, really? I don't give a damn about international law right now. I think you're missing the big picture here. If what the Admiral said is true. That dad's predictions are starting to come true; don't you know what that means. For us, for the planet? I mean they didn't call him the doomsday doctor for nothing. I should be helping dad, not spying on him."

"Yes, it's true. Your father made a lot of bold predictions, but it doesn't quite mean the end of the world. Not yet any way."

"Mom, it sounds like you're siding with them."

"I'm not siding with anyone right now. There's a lot at stake here Tom. The future of our country may be at risk."

The Chinese aren't exactly our friends Tom."

"Well from where I'm sitting, our government aren't exactly our friends either. Remember what happened at the Island? Someone killed Dale and Buffy and kidnapped my students. And our government may have been partly responsible."

"I know, dear. You have a point. I just don't see that we have a lot of options right now. But they may not let us go unless we cooperate."

Polly was silently listening, while she slowly ate, and watched as a group of starlings danced in the summer sun.

Looking first at Kate and then at Tom she said, "You know Tom, you haven't seen your dad in a long time. It wouldn't hurt to talk to him."

Just then Admiral Goldsby cleared his throat as he approached the back patio, "There sure is a nice view here. Mind if I join you for a few minutes?"

Polly got up and said, "You can have my seat Mike, I'm going up stairs to take a shower. She cleared the plates as she left, leaving the three of them alone."

For a brief moment Tom saw one of the Seal Team protecting the house move into his line of sight from behind a tree. And he realized how serious the situation was. If not for the Admiral, they might be shackled to a dirty basement floor being waterboarded right now."

The Admiral looked at Tom and said, "Son, we are all on the same team here. I realize how upset you must be. I'm not going to give you the "your country needs you speech." But, that's kinda the situation here. We really need intel on your father's activities. If you can think of another way, I'm willing to listen. But right now, you're our only option."

Gaining some determination, Tom looked the general in the eye and said, "I'll do what I can, but I want my mom out of this. She stays here at the farm, under your protection. Polly stays with me. She's already proved herself to be invaluable in a tight spot and right now she's the only one I can trust. No offence. I'm just a little wary of the "government cooperation thing right now."

The Admiral motioned for an aid who was standing off in the distance, and said, "I was hoping you would say that. I was going to recommend that Polly be part of your detail anyway. I just need you to sign some paperwork, just a formality of course. We'll go over the details of your mission; um I mean your trip in route. We have plenty of time. It's a long flight to New Zealand."

CHAPTER 16

John was just finishing his speech at the UN Climate Change Conference in New York, when there was a loud explosion. The lights went out as the protestors stormed the conference and room and began chanting, "Coal today, coal tomorrow, coal forever!" As the emergency lighting came on, John was whisked off stage by UN security personal and he and Kate were ushered out a side entrance and into a waiting UN security van.

The limo that was waiting for them outside the front entrance was then rerouted to another venue. While in route, the car was stopped on a busy railway by an overturned semi. And before the driver could back up, the car was hit by an Eastbound train and cut in half.

John and Kate returned to their hotel and as they got to their suite, Kate put on the TV hoping for an update on the UN conference protests. What they saw on the local news horrified them both as they watched "on the scene" coverage of the limo / train accident. The images showed the limo cut in half and turned upside down in a fiery crash. When the coverage cut back to the studio and reported the drivers name with his picture, they realized that it was the driver of the limo assigned to them.

Clutching John's arm Kate said, "John, wasn't that our driver?"

"Yes, I believe it was," he said as he looked out the hotel window at the street below. "That was no coincidence. I was supposed to die in that crash, and you with me. Maybe you're right. This is getting to be too much."

With a tear in her eye she looked at John and said, "What are we going to do now?"

He said, "Let's check with your sister and make sure little Tom is ok. Maybe we should keep him out of school, until we get back, then I don't know. Kate, I can't just give up my research. Besides, we can't be absolutely sure that wasn't just an accident."

She turned and grabbed him by the arm and looking into his eyes said, "John, a man died. That was no accident. The safety gate didn't even activate. They tried to kill us today for Christs sake John! What's it going to take for you to realize the forces you're up against are just too powerful."

He reached out to hug her and as she pushed him away, he said, "I don't know, what if we go into hiding?"

Kate went to a side table where she poured herself a drink from a crystal pitcher and said, "I can't live like that. Tom has already missed too much school. There is nowhere to go that they can't find us. I'm sure there are other projects you could work on for now. Then in the fall, you can start over again on something new."

"Kate, I can't unbreak this egg. You know what's at stake. If I don't continue my work who will? We presented our findings. There is no disputing the science. They will have to act. The future of the human race in jeopardy."

Openly crying now, Kate said through tears, "John, you can't do anything if you're dead."

Looking at Kate with a glint in his eye he said, "What if they just think I'm dead?"

Looking away Kate said, "John you can't be serious."

"I don't know what else to do. If they think I'm dead, they'll have to leave us alone."

Kate sat on the love seat facing John and said, "Come on John, think about it. How are you going to continue your research if everyone thinks you're dead? The government is not going to be thrilled by your speech you know. They sure as hell aren't putting you in witness protection or anything."

He said, "I know Kate, but if you thought things were bad before. It's only going to get worse now. I don't see any other way."

"Well what about Tommy? You can't just fake your death and leave us behind. And where would you go? Wherever it is, if you're in hiding, we can't go with you."

"What about New Zealand? I was born there. I'm sure I could hide out with some of my old friends until this blow over. It's far from prying eyes. Once I get set up there, you and Tommy could move, and we could get away from all this."

"John, think this through. What about *my* research? I have 10 research assistants on my payroll and I'm two years into a five-year research project. I can't just give up my grants and move halfway around the world. And even if I could. What about my family? I can't just leave them behind. My mom's in a nursing home, she needs me John. I'm sorry but it's just too far away."

With real concern in his voice he said, "I'm serious Kate, don't know what else to do."

Kate said, "I know you're desperate, but that's just going too far."

John said, "Desperate times call for desperate measures. My death might be the only way I can live to save mankind. You almost died today too Kate. Next time we might not be so lucky. We can't risk our future on luck. We have to get ahead of this.

Six months later, John's car slid off the rain slick Pacific Coast Highway and crashed into the sea. His body was never found, and he was declared dead. After staging the crash with the help of a friend from the engineering department, he was smuggled across the border by a former research assistant. He made his way down to Rocky Point Mexico, where he hopped a fishing boat to Puerto Vallarta. Traveling with just a backpack, and using a burner phone, he contacted a pair of former research assistants working at the University of Guadalajara.

Dave and Holly Fontaine hadn't changed much since he'd last seen them 10 years ago at Mexico City conference. They picked him up just outside of Itapúa, as he was sitting in the shade at an outdoor café. As planned, they pulled up in their beat-up pickup truck to the local gas station and he hopped in the back under an old tarp as Dave filled up the old truck with gas, and Holly went to use the facilities.

John had worked with the Fontane's, back in the 70s at UCS where he was a visiting adjunct professor in the school of eco-sciences. Dave and Holly were in love; with each other and with the sciences. They had both spent 10 years in the military. Dave in clandestine system operations and Holly in advanced communication technologies. They both met at USC and it was John that sparked their interest in ecology and eco-sciences. He found their combined skills most valuable, when it came to finding things people, and organizations didn't want found.

Now of course, John needed their special skill set once again.

A few miles out of town they pulled over and John got in the cab next to Holly. The buxom blond gave John a welcome back hug and kiss as they pulled back on the one lane dirt road. Dave, never surprised by John's eccentricity, laughed as they pulled away.

"So, what have you gotten yourself into now?" Dave said as they bumped along the well-worn dirt road.

"Well, let's get to the house first. Did you get the stuff I asked for?" John said as he downed the beer Holly had just handed him.

"Yeah we got it. Most of it anyway," said Holly snuggling up to John and holding his hand.

"Here," she said as she handed him a bottle of tequila, John took a swig and felt the warm glow of the golden liquid permeate his essence like water poured into hot sand.

Lost in their own thoughts, they were silent as they truck bumped along the dusty road. Dave thought John looked scared and desperate, and that was not John's nature. Something must have really spooked him. All alone, on the run with just the clothes on his back. Something was very wrong, and Dave worried for his old friend.

As they bounced down dirt road the oppressive 95-degree heat bore down on John like a mud sandwich. He hadn't eaten or slept in nearly 3 days. He insisted on pulling over every 5 miles or so, hiding on an off-road ditch or back-way, looking out for pursuers. He was confident he got away clean but had a distinct feeling like he was being watched. They got to Guadalajara without incident. And after a hot shower and a great dinner of pork tacos with rice and beans, they sat out on the veranda and after a few margaritas John unfolded his story.

"It all started when I discovered the global warming / climate change cover up. He said nervously holding his glass like a challis. After I gave the keynote speech at the UN Climate Change Summit, our limo got hit by a train, the driver was killed, but by a stroke of good luck we weren't in the car."

"After that I was blacklisted. Remember the climate change summit in Vienna? You know, the one I planned for two years? Well

1st of all, my conference credentials were canceled. For Christ's sake, Dave, I set the whole thing up. I was the keynote speaker! Then my flight was canceled, not just my ticket but the whole flight! It was a chartered flight and when I called the airline, their number was no longer in service, it was not a working number. They'd been bought out. All their planes were sold, and the business dissolved. I thought for a minute I was losing my mind. Then I found out my passport had been held back. Restricted, I wasn't even allowed to leave the country. "A Travel risk" was I all I could get from the state dept. I called and got passed around and put on hold for hours at a time. I finally just gave up. When I talked to my attorney, you know, Hal? My wife's cousin. He wouldn't even take my calls. Shit, I've known him for 30 yrs. We went to Oxford together. He introduced me to Kate.

Then I met with the University governing board. They said they needed to see me regarding an urgent matter. They said they wanted me out, but since they couldn't fire a tenured professor, they just eliminated my department. They defunded my research projects, throwing 15 researchers on the street. Can you imagine? Stanford University without a climate science department? Then they closed my office. I went in the next day and it was all boarded up. Not just my office but the whole fucking building. Closed for renovation. Renovation! Shit, it was built in 1896, they've been renovating that dam building forever. So, I thought well, I'll just take a sabbatical until all this nonsense blows over. My request for a sabbatical was denied. They even took my parking space away.

Then I found our house phone was tapped and my home office was bugged. And I kept getting these late-night calls. Threatening me with blackmail. Blackmail! I said go to hell, I've never had any-thing to hide. They sent me doctored photos of someone who kinda looked like me at a gay bar with a young man. Hell, Jill knows I've been gay for 20 yrs. So, I said go ahead, when that didn't work, they went after my family. My wife's research grant was canceled. Then the bank foreclosed on our house. We hadn't missed a payment in 25 yrs. Then and our dog went missing, and we had a break in. They really trashed the place looking for something. I mean these guys had it in for me. I have no proof, but I'm pretty sure I know who they are, I just can't prove anything, yet. So now I'm in hiding. I didn't know what else to do. I mean if they think I'm dead…

Dave looked incredulously at his old friend, "What do you mean if they think you're dead? John what are you saying?"

Well, I don't know how to say this but, I'm legally dead. At least I think so. My car crashed off a cliff into the ocean off the Pacific Coast Hwy. With nobody, I figured they'd have to declare me dead eventually.

Dave was so startled he spilled his drink and almost knocked over the table. "Oh my god! John," he said……." you gotta be shitting me……your dead? I mean like dead and gone. When you said you had to get away for a while, I mean, I … we thought you just needed a break, you know a little R&R, a vacation. John what the hell's going on?"

Looking around the South American countryside John said, "Like I told you someone is out to get me."

The next morning Dave was up early and put together a specialized laptop for John. He installed a specialized network algorithm that would bounce his signal off literally hundreds of computers masking any attempts to isolate his location or network address. Then Dave made John a new identity with ID cards a passport and credit cards.

With Dave's help, John accessed bank accounts he had spread around the world where he stashed most of his vast fortune. His parents had left him with a nice inheritance, but it was the patents he created while still a research assistant at MIT, that made him a very wealthy man. As a graduate assistant he was researching the effects of bacteria on wastewater treatment plants, when he made a significant breakthrough in water treatment technology. The bacteria that he created and patented were now used in nearly every water treatment facility across the globe. The accounts he set up around the world just kept cashing checks and reinvesting the money in emerging technologies. Some of his accounts he hadn't looked at in years and he was surprised to learn that his net worth was close to a billion dollars.

With Dave's help, John made his way to New Zealand, where he enlisted the help of his old boyhood friend.

CHAPTER 17

Wearing a clever disguise and using his fake credentials, John leased a private jet and flew to Queenstown, New Zealand where he met up with his old boyhood friend Rusty Otis. John knew Rusty from his childhood and Rusty was one of his oldest and closest friends. They used to camp, hunt and fish together in the New Zealand wilderness. Whereas John went to the US to get an education, Rusty followed in his family tradition of sheep farming.

When John contacted Rusty, he was more than happy to do whatever he could to help out his old friend, any excuse to get off the farm he told John more than once.

Following John's instructions, Rusty had been searching for a suitable location for the factory John plan to build. He needed a place away from any major cities with a supply of freshwater preferably in a valley surrounded by mountains.

His request was a tall order. Although New Zealand had plenty of undeveloped areas, most of the country was divided into two large islands, protected as national parks or wetlands. After three weeks of searching plot maps at the local library, they rented a helicopter and scoured the countryside in search of the perfect place to build a secret factory.

Over several bottles of wine at the hotel restaurant, Rusty jokingly said, "Too bad we can't just buy our own island."

Lost in his own thoughts, John quipped, "I thought you said, we should buy our own island."

Rusty got up and stretched and said, "Yeah, don't you remember when we were Kids. We used to play Pirates and pretend we had our own Island. John, I know you've been gone awhile, but a couple years ago the country got into some financial trouble. They put Three Kings Island up for sale, but dey got no takers. It's just a hunk of rock a couple miles off the North Shore. Trouble is, there's nothing there, no ports, no airport, no power, no nothin mate. The island hasn't changed since the abos first came to this country 20,000 years ago."

John downed his beer, got up from the table, and said to Rusty, "My friend, that sounds perfect how much you think they want for the place?"

Rusty, thinking John had had a little too much to drink just laughed and said, "Don't know mate, I'm sure we can find out. I'll give my sister a call tomorrow, she works at the deserted island store. Laughing he motioned to the waitress for another round and headed to the bathroom.

As John steadied himself on one of the old wooden high back chairs surrounding the table he said, "Rusty old boy, I›m as serious as a heart attack."

Rusty, still making fun of his drunk friend said as he stumbled off to the bathroom, "Well I›ll be a stuffed wallaby, why didn›t you just say you wanted to buy your own Island, could have saved us a lot of time."

John woke early, a little hungover from too many Speights beers, and knocking on Rusty's hotel room door said, "Come along boy, we got an island to buy."

Rusty woke up from a sound sleep, threw his boot at the door and said, "I›ll meet you at the bar for a bloody in 15."

John was helping himself to the breakfast buffet when Rusty made his way up to the bar. He ordered a Bloody Mary with a beer chaser and waited for John to join him on one of the empty bar stools.

Rusty said as he downed a big gulp from the fiery red liquid, "What›s all this about buying an island?"

John said, "Quit kidding around, I'm serious. Just how do we go about getting on the island to check it out."

Rusty said, "If you›re really serious I›ve got a cousin who works for the Parks Department, I'm pretty sure she'll be able to steer us in the right direction."

As John drank the hair of the dog from his Speight beer bottle he said between mouthfuls of food, "Well let›s get a move on, if we›re going to save the world, we've got a lot to do. Hey, you going to have anything to eat, the buffet here is pretty good?"

Rusty downed his Bloody Mary and asked for another and said to John, "You're serious about this island shit, aren't you?"

John looked Rusty in the eye and said, "Serious as a heart attack mate. If you're not going to eat brunch, you best skip the Bloody Mary, you're driving remember?"

Rusty said, as he got up and went to the bathroom. "What the hell, you sound like my ex-wife." He yelled, "Hey barkeep make that one for the road, choice, oi."

Starting with the parks department they got bounced around from one agency to the next until finally they made an appointment to see the assistant to the Assistant Prime Minister.

It took 3 days, but they were finally waiting in the outer office and Rusty said to John, "You know mate, it's too bad we're not back in the pirate days. "We could just sail in and capture the island for ourselves."

John looked at his old friend and said, you know Rusty that might not be such a bad idea. These bureaucrats sure don't know their ass from a hole in the ground, by the time they get around to making any kind of decision it's going to be too late."

Rusty said, "You're right about that mate. They're about as slow as maple syrup in July."

John said, "don't you mean January."

Rusty said, looking up at the antique upside-down world map on the wall said, "You old fool, you been at the bottom of the world too long, our winters from March to October."

John smiled and looking at Rusty said, "Yeah I guess you're right, things are different down here, aren't they?"

John got up and paced the small anteroom looking at the wall sized world map and noticing it was upside down relative to the Northern hemisphere and said," Does New Zealand have a navy or even an air force?"

Sitting comfortably in the soft leather chair rusty said, "I sure could go for a smoke mate, you got a fag? Yeah-no, they ain't got no navy or air force here. We're a British Commonwealth doggie. We are a protectorate of the queen herself. The Queen of England that is. The British Navy has some ships down 'ere and the Air Force some planes but it's mostly for show. The blokes I know, spend most of der time in the pubs chasing skirts an getting drunk on the Queen's dime."

Just then, a very pretty secretary, wearing a short skirt and tight blouse came in and said, Mr. Ballentine will see you now."

She walked towards the large wooden door guarding the entrance to the assistant of the Assistant Prime Minister's office and as she opened the ornate door said, "Right this way gentlemen."

She held the door open for them as they entered a large well-appointed office suite. A very round and very well-dressed Mr. Ballentine got up from his desk, and as he approached the two men, shook their hands and guided them towards the two antique chairs positioned strategically in front of his large antique desk.

John immediately noticed the man's presidential gold Rolex, Armani suit and solid gold cufflinks. John had heard rumors of the culture of graft and bribery in the land down under; 10,000 miles from the Queen's guard. In fact, he was counting on it.

Mr. Ballentine made a show of casually walking around the large desk and sitting in a custom leather desk chair and he said in a thick Kiwi accent, "Good day, gentleman. How can ay be of service, oi. My calendar says that you have some interest in Kings Island?"

Suddenly feeling a little uncomfortable, as if he was sitting in the principal's office and grade school, John said, "Yes sir, your majesty sir, I mean, Mr. Ballentine. I had heard that the island was for sale, is that true?"

Mr. Ballentine's face formed a phony bureaucratic smile, as he leaned back in his chair and said, "Wherever did you get such a daft idea?"

Squirming uncomfortably in his chair, John stole a glance at Rusty and said, "That's what I heard your honor sir, it must have been a rumor."

Mr. Ballentine, the scent of graft in the air said, "What on earth could you possibly want with that lonely rock?"

John said, I›m a scientist from America and I›m looking for a location to build a research facility and factory, away from prying eyes if you will. I›ve gone over the maps and did a flyover, and it doesn›t appear that anyone actually lives on the island, isn›t that correct?"

Mr. Ballentine leaned forward taking a large cigar from a small humidor on his desk. He methodically went through the process of cutting and lighting the large cigar with a 14-karat gold lighter, blowing smoke towards the ornate 15 ft tin ceiling, where a fan above his desk swirled the smoke high above his head.

As he watched the smoke dissipate, he said, "You're telling me that you want to build a factory, on a deserted island in the South Pacific, thousands of miles from any kind of major supply chain, on an island with no seaport or infrastructure of any kind? Not only do you want to build a factory on this island, do you want to buy the island. I'm not sure you're aware of this my good man but, I'm sorry I didn't get your last name, oh yeah, it's right here. Mr. Nash. We don't allow foreigners to buy land in New Zealand."

John, a little put back by the man's demeanor, would not be deterred. Well, Mr. Ballentine, John said as he pulled out a notepad, "Would you consider a long-term lease arrangement. For those in the chain of command, if you will, could have the inside track to some very lucrative stock options, and a 6-figure signing bonus. These kinds of deals are done all the time in the corporate world. As long as we're not violating any laws of the crown of course."

"Well, that changes things a wee bit," said Mr. Ballentine, as he leaned back in his chair and puffed on his oversized cigar.

Rolling the cigar in his thick fingers, he said, "The islands in question are outside the territorial authority of New Zealand and are listed with the New Zealand Outlying Islands under the direction of the Department of the Interior. My cousin 'appens to be the assistant director to the Minister of the Interior himself. I could make some calls on your behalf. But I have a very busy schedule as you can imagine."

John wrote a number on the notepad and showed it to Mr. Ballentine and putting his cigar in a gold-plated ashtray said, "It looks like my schedule just freed up."

John, pulling an envelope with $10,000 out of his suit jacket, said, "This should cover any um, administrative expenses. I'm staying in a suite at the Lodge at Kauri Cliffs unit 2100. Here's my local cell. We are under a strict deadline, to secure a location, or I'll have to review other options."

Mr. Ballentine, reached across the table, took the envelope and dropped it into his top desk drawer and said, "It just so 'appens that I'm having dinner with my cousin tonight. I'm sure I can 'ave an answer for you in the morrow."

"I'm just curious," said Mr. Ballantine, as he rose from his chair, signaling that the meeting was over. "What do you plan on making in this factory of yours?"

Rusty and John got up from their chairs and as they turned to walk out John said, "Toys Mr. Ballentine, very expensive toys."

After meeting with the assistant to the assistant of the Interior Minister, and presenting a cashier's check for $100,000, with a 100-year lease in his hand, John was ready to begin construction of his secret factory on the Three Kings Islands.

Over drinks at the local pub, Rusty raised his mug and said, "I've got to hand it to ya mate, you pulled that one off without a hitch. But for the life of me, I cannot fathom why you want to go and build a factory out of solid rock on an island in the middle of nowhere without so much as a pot to piss in, has your head started to rot from the inside out?"

John openly laughed for the first time in months, and he raised his glass meeting Rusty's, and said, "Rusty old boy, have I ever let you down?"

Rusty downed his beer and motioned for another round and said, "No, I s'pose not, but you got me wonderin. You know my family 'as got about 2,000 acres of perfectly good valley land. Flat you know, easy to build stuff on. Freshwater lake. Off the main road. All the lamb you can stomach, if you know what I mean. The family ain't much for sheep'n no more. Most only doing it cause they don't know how ta do notin else."

John ordered a picture of beer, grabbed his case full of maps and charts and took Rusty in the back room, and as he closed the door, he said, "I'll let you in on a little secret. Remember when we did that fly over of the island, and you said, "Ain't nothing down there but a little volcano, not enough flatland to even land a helicopter on."

Rusty took a bit out of a deep-fried turkey leg and said, "So, what's your point?"

John opened his case and took out a chart of the Island chain. As he flattened the curled edges of the geological survey map, he said, "Take a look at this. I had a survey done on the island and found that this volcanic formation along this continental rift in the ocean floor, created this island chain separately from New Zealand. So, in other words, this is a completely different and distinct geological formation then either New Zealand or Australia. Underneath what we see as the volcano structure, is actually a dome of basaltic rock. And the same is true for the separate Islands in this chain. The island itself is 2 miles across it has a natural harbor on the southwest side, and the height at the top of the dome is about 900 ft. Which means that the interior of the volcanic dome should measure about 10 million cubic yards."

As he poured another beer, Rusty said, "Yeah nay, so how's it choice mate? It still looks like a big hunk of rock to me?"

Pulling out another map, John said, 'It's not what's on top that I'm interested in. It's what's underneath. Haven't you been listening? Ok look at it this way. You know the Rod Laver Stadium in Sydney? It holds about 20,000 people."

Chewing on another turkey wing Rusty said, "Yeah-na so?"

"Well imagine a stadium 1000 times bigger. That's what we have here, underneath this rock dome." John said as he leaned back against the wall. "I can't think of a better place to build a secret factory, then a place no one would ever look."

A light went on in Rusty's head and he said, "Sweet as, now I get it. You gonna build a factory underground, is that it?"

"You got it now mate," John said as he pointed to the SW corner of the main island and said, "See this inlet here, it's a natural harbor. We start construction there. Once that's complete, then we can bring in all the heavy machinery we need for the rest of the project."

Rusty, having worked in the construction industry in Australia for several years said, "Yeah-nah, that's gonna take years, mate. What are ya gonna do till then?"

John pulling out another map said, "You were saying something about your family farm?"

CHAPTER 18

After an Otis clan meeting, all 72 of them, save a few, held at the local union hall, it was agreed that they would lease a good portion of their valley to LRC, aka. the Loveton Robotic Corp.

And soon after, John began the construction of the first robotic factory in the world, dedicated to the design and manufacture of the robots which would be used to complete the construction of the interior of King's Island.

With Rusty's assistance, John went to the largest construction company in Australia and signed a multi-year contract to develop the Kings Island project. The company, having built high rise hotels, hydroelectric dams, long span bridges, and nuclear power plants, was the perfect fit the scope of the Kings Island project.

Based on his initial designs the project was scheduled to take at least five years, and included; a port and docking system, a water collection and waste treatment plant, a light rail system, a small nuclear power plant and the construction and build out of the dome interior.

In the interim, John made use of the Otis family sheep farm to build the first stage of robots designed specifically for the underground construction of the Kings Island project.

Rusty's family, which had raised sheep for 5 generations in the same valley, was happy to sell out to the newly formed Loveton Robotic Corp. Over the years, less and less of the family were interested in following the family tradition, although, New Zealand wool was still in high demand, the younger generation wasn't interested in the long hours and boring work associated with sheep husbandry.

While John's team of engineers repurposed the inner valley farms and began construction of the first phase of the robotic factory. The outer valley livestock farms were kept in operation to keep up appearances.

Making use of robotic technology used in the auto industry, Loveton bought out the robotics platform from a closed auto plant in the US and had the whole assembly line shipped to New Zealand and brought to the new factory operation at the Otis farmstead.

CHAPTER 19

Using his new identity and cleverly designed disguises, John traveled the world and encouraged carefully selected scientists and researchers to join him in New Zealand in a quest to save humanity.

With his scientific and international connections, and with the assistance of several of the world's most noted scientists, he initiated a secret project. Code named the Evolution Project. The Evolution Project would take years to reach fruition. The goal of his project was to construct several large and self-sustaining space colonies. And secretly move the chosen few to the inhospitable refuge of space!

CHAPTER 20

John's research indicated that small Island countries around the world would be the first tragic victims of advanced climate change when irreversible glacial melting occurs around the globe flooding their small home islands.

He encouraged many of the younger members to leave their Island homes and move to the Otis family farm. There, he employed, and trained them in his robotic factory. Where under his direction they built robots of the future. Robots designed to work independently designing and building advanced AI humanoids.

John, with the help of his team of engineers, architects and designers build an infrastructure for everything they needed for their future plans. They started with excavating rare earth minerals, then built solar, geothermal, ocean wave and natural gas power plants. Next, they concentrated on building a camouflaged industrial complex the size of four football fields, with near zero emissions.

Advances made by John's team of structural engineers and advanced software designers exceeded even John's wildest dreams. Driven by a burning desire to save mankind from the fate of extinction, they worked tirelessly day and night, breaking barriers and creating systems and technologies that were light years ahead of anything done before.

In the span of five years, working day and night, the team was able to complete the construction of the first humanoid robotic prototype. The missing piece to the puzzle, was an industrial size robotic carbon fiber nanotube 3D printer.

Once the main infrastructure of the dome was completed. The build out of the dome interior continued using robotic 3-D printers and the city scape became the prototype for the interior of the habisphere project.

CHAPTER 21

Tom and Polly flew via helicopter, first to Norfolk Naval Base, then on a CIA Gulfstream jet to the North Island Naval Air Station San Diego, CA.

At the tech lab Tom was outfitted with state-of-the-art surveillance equipment. A microchip was embedded in his scalp that would record everything he heard. Not one to wear ear jewelry, Tom was fitted with an earring and stud that provided video capture. He was also provided with a watch fitted with a GPS transponder, Bluetooth and two-way communicator. As he was shown how to work the ultra-sleek watch, he thought his James Bond reference, wasn't so off the mark.

After leaving the lab, Tom was taken to a secure conference room where he was briefed by a team assembled by Admiral Goldsby. Everyone around a large oval conference table was sitting watching a video display of Kings Island. As Tom entered the room, Admiral Goldsby said, "Tom, just the man we want to see. We were just going over the latest data from King's Island. Let me introduce Jill Hillenbrand. She is our lead researcher on this, and I'll let her get you caught up to speed."

And as he rotated in seat he said, "Jill you're up."

Jill stood and said as she activated a remote-controlled wall size screen. "Here is a satellite photo of King's Island. As we zoom in on this corner of the island, we can see a state-of-the-art shipping port and docking system. It took us a year to reposition a specialized spy satellite to this part of the globe with enough magnification to provide these detailed photos." As she zoomed in on the port she said, "Now just to clarify what we're seeing here. This port is fully automated, and I mean fully. There are no people in this area at all."

Someone at the far end of the table interrupted, and said, "What do you mean, there are clearly 4 people on the ground right there."

"Yes," she said, "so it appears. That's why we needed the sat upgrade. As we zoom in at higher resolution, we can see that what appears to be human beings, are in fact advanced robots. In all outward appearance, they appear to be as human as you and I. It was only after we analyzed the infrared spectrum, we saw this."

The next slide was a close up of the post and showed almost no heat signature at all. "Not what we should be seeing here, in the infrared are reds, blues and greens. Not greys." at first we thought our $200 million dollar satellite had taken a dump. However, after a rigorous shake down we determined the set was fully functional. Applying Jacobs Razor, the premises that the simplest answer, 9 times out of ten is the right one. We could only assume that LRC has taken a giant step forward in robotic technology."

"Now people, I can't emphasize enough what we are seeing here. This is like something out of the movie Terminator come to life. This tech is light years ahead of anything, anywhere on the planet. In addition, these robots appear to be completely self-autonomous. In other words, they appear to be completely free thinking. We've all read about the future of AI, or artificial intelligence. The good and the bad and what the implications of that entail. Well people, like or not, the future of AI is alive and here today on King's Island."

"There are those at the highest level in our military that see King's Island as an existential threat to world peace. And, that the technology we are about to see, will disrupt the delicate balance between the world's superpowers for years to come."

Another hand went up from someone at the table. Jill turned and said, "Yes?"

"Yes, um, Tim Sanders here, from NASA. How could a tiny little island, in the middle of nowhere, be a threat to world peace."

Jill stepped forward and said, "You may now open the folders in front of you. The file you are about to see is classified so top secret, we are not even allowed to have it on our server here, and after this briefing, these documents will be destroyed under guard in blast furnace at 3,000 degrees."

As a group, and with some apprehension, they opened the folders and Jill said, "As you can see from these photos, after some difficulty, we were able to gain access to the island, although we paid dearly for it. The team that was able to infiltrate the island's security, obtained these pictures using stealth drones."

"What we see here in the first few pics are flying robotic soldiers. Yes, you heard me correctly. These units are fully weaponized and outfitted with full body armor. The weapon technology being deployed here is something our top scientists are still trying to figure out. Two of these things, took down an entire squad of our most elite soldiers without firing a shot. One minute our forces were engaging the target, the next thing they remember is waking up in custody. If that wasn't bad enough. As if to poke us in the eye. The entire team was transported directly to the White House lawn under the cover of darkness, without alerting a single US security agency. Including White House security."

"If you will now turn to section 3a of your folder, you can see security video footage of the helicopter pad located on the White House lawn. One second nothing, then all of a sudden, poof they just seem to appear out of nowhere. Somehow, they took out an elite team of our best soldiers, using an advanced weapon that rendered them unconscious, and erased their memory. Then, somehow, they were flown 12,000 miles, halfway around the globe. Evading the most advanced security system in the world and landed them on the White House lawn without a trace."

"There are those in the military that want this island nuked, as a threat to national security. They feel that any army as advanced as this, is a serious threat to world peace."

As she looked around the room, she said, "Any questions?"

No one looked up from the table as Jill moved on to the next file. When she said, "You may now open the second folder in front of you." Everyone did as instructed and Jill waited until the last folder was opened.

"Again, this file is restricted at the highest level. These photos are of the second volcano in the King's Island chain, where the LRC aka the Loveton Robotic Corporation has its secret satellite launch system. We don't have pictures of the actual launch, due to a disruption in our satellite surveillance system. Yes, it was hacked. The next series of photos are from ground-based telescopes of the satellite, and what it morphed into, yes I said morphed."

"This again is something so far advanced, our researchers are trying to figure out how this is happening. In the 72 hours since the deployment of the craft, it has built this. And she held up a 36x24 inch poster showing what looked like the internal frame of an aircraft carrier. This thing is already twice the size of the ISS (international space station.)

Murmurs could be heard around the room as Admiral Goldsby stood and said, "Thank you Ms. Hillenbrand. As you are all aware, nothing from this meeting leaves this room. Now I ask that you clear the room. Tom, you will come with me. We have another meeting scheduled with our partners at the NSA and DARPA."

Tom was escorted through a maze of office corridors and taken out a side exit into a waiting military SUV, with an armed escort. Tom and Admiral Goldsby were in the back seat and Tom turned to speak. The Admiral held his hand up and said, "Don't speak here. We're on our way to another safe room. I got a message that we were compromised back at the base. An advanced AI computer system has been probing our network. We think your dad might be responsible. We need to finish your briefing and get you and Polly on a plane to New Zealand ASAP. A State Department envoy will be meeting us at the Auckland airport tomorrow our time. You will actually get there today, but it will be tomorrow here, Earth's rotation and all, never mind.

Tom and Polly arrived at the US embassy in Auckland, at 9 am local time. Tom slept most of the 12-hour flight and the rest did him some good. The Embassy was almost exactly as Tom expected. An old, gaudy, ornate building in the center of the city. Under heavy security, they were ushered in a side entrance, and brought to their sleeping quarters. Which to Tom's surprise were extremely comfortable.

The US State Department, through the New Zealand Interior Ministry, contacted King's Island and Tom and Polly were invited to the island as honored guests.

They were flown on a LRC helicopter to King's Island and Tom and Polly were greeted at the flight terminal by Crystal, a tall, very attractive 20 something blond. She introduced herself as one of John's personal assistants before she started their tour she gave both

Tom and Polly a fashionable smartwatch that she said took the place of a smartphone here at King's Island. A small autonomous shuttle pulled up and Crystal gestured towards the rear seats. Tom and Polly took their seats and the car sped away and into a small tunnel cut into the side of the volcanic dome which brought them into a monorail hub connected to the vast interior.

Tom was overwhelmed by the immense scope of the island's infrastructure. It was a bit like walking through the Emerald City in the Wizard of OZ.

There were monorails and moving sidewalks everywhere. Drones, flying in organized flight paths were moving goods around the dome like something out of a science fiction movie. Then Tom realized. Science fiction were just advances in technology that haven't happened yet. He remembered a quote, from somewhere that, "Any sufficiently advanced technology was indistinguishable from magic." And, "The only way of discovering the limits of the possible, is to venture a little way past them into the impossible." He thought his father had indeed moved from the impossible to the possible.

Tom and Polly felt a bit like royalty as they were escorted through the maze-like central city of the LRC headquarters. Even though the entire structure was underground, the lighting from a sun like system that moved across the dome had the effect like the sun rising and setting in the sky and made it seem like real daylight. To add to the illusion, the top of the dome was ingeniously painted to look like the sky on a bright summer day and had a rising and setting moon and twinkling stars by night.

As they continued on their tour, Tom was constantly amazed by the design of the interior. He expected to see lava rocks and stalactites. Instead there were parks and trees growing everywhere with insects and birds flying here and there. Waterfalls and streams seemed to appear out of nowhere as they walked through the sculptured landscape. When they passed a small lake at one end of the underground city, a fish jumped out of the water. When they stopped for lunch at an outdoor cafe, for the moment, they forgot they were hundreds of feet under the dome of a giant volcano.

Tom was so immersed in the experience, he completely forgot about the surveillance equipment he was wearing. Nothing could have prepared him for the immense planning that went into the construction and design of the interior of the domed city. There were stores and restaurants a movie theater and even a bowling alley.

Following the tour, Tom and Polly were shown to their sleeping quarters. Every modern convenience was thoughtfully designed into a seemingly organic construction that looked like appliances and furniture just sprouted out of the ground.

Polly was shown to a separate suite while Tom was shown his. As he walked into the well-appointed suite, the AI system that monitored Kings Island spoke as if from nowhere. Tom was startled as the AI said, "Welcome to Kings Island Mr. Loveton. My name is Adam, I will serve as your personal assistant, and can answer most of your questions."

Tom realized that the voice he was hearing wasn't coming from a speaker or sound system but was in his head. At first, he thought his implant had been hacked, then the AI assistant said, "You're probably wondering where my voice is coming from. I am vibrating the tympani bone in your inner ear with subsonic vibrations. Only you can hear me."

A little shocked at the perceived intrusion to his personal space, Tom said, "Do you communicate with everyone this way?"

"Yes, the voice said, "You will get used to it. It's a bit like having your own set of personal headphones, without having to wear anything. If you like music, I can play your favorite artists or musical styles, or you can choose from any book ever written and I can read it to you in any voice you choose. I can even answer any question you have about virtually anything, the entire internet is at your disposal, all you have to do is ask."

"Can I turn you off?" Tom asked somewhat annoyed by the sudden intrusion into his personal space.

"Yes," Adam said. "However, it is part of my function to monitor all activities on Kings Island."

"Even in the bedroom?" Tom said.

"Yes, I am present everywhere. I'm sorry if you are bothered by my presence. Most of our guests are not aware of the full extent of my function. Your father thought it was essential that you were aware of every aspect of King's Island."

"Speaking of my father, where is he. I have lots of questions only he can answer."

"Yes, I'm sure you do. He is busy at the moment; however, he is anxious to meet with you over dinner. Why don't you relax. I can have anything you desire brought to your room. You must still be jet lagged from your trip, may I suggest a hot tub and a bottle of wine."

"How do I reach Polly?"

"She is in the suite down the hall. If you like I can call her room."

"Does she know about you?"

"No, at your father's request. I was instructed to make my presence known only to you."

"How do I reach her?"

"There are comm links all over the complex."

"What do they look like. I don't see what looks like phone anywhere."

"Of course, I should have showed you earlier. The watch you are wearing is fitted with a micro communication device. All you have to do is say, "Call Polly", and I will connect you to her."

"How will she hear me, through that inner ear bone like now?"

"Yes, all auditory communication is done through this method. As I said before. You will get used to it. It's the same, with most of our guests."

"Ok. Call Polly."

Sounding much like switchboard operator Adam said, "One moment while I connect you."

Seeming to come out of nowhere and everywhere all at once, Polly's voice erupted in his head. "Tom, Hi. It's me Polly. I'm in the hot tub right now. Isn't this place wonderful? It's like the MIT, NASA and Disney World all rolled into one. And isn't this communication technology the best. DARPA has nothing like it I'm sure."

"Yes, it's incredible Polly. Everything in the place is like something out of a science fiction novel."

"I'm going to finish my bath and then take a nap if you want to join me wink wink."

"Look Polly, there's something you should know."

All at once, the comm link dropped and Adam said, "Tom. You are asked not to reveal my presence to anyone at this time. You father's instructions. Polly knows me as Sheila, her personal AI assistant."

"Ok I get, it put me through."

"Of course."

"Tom helloooo, are you there?"

"Yes, Polly I'm here. I'll take a rain check on that nap. I'm going to rest in my room for a while. I'll come by your room before dinner."

And with that, the communication ended. "I'm sorry," Adam said, "about the intrusion, however, I was given strict instructions. You are one of only a handful of staff that know of my existence."

"You said that my dad wanted me to have knowledge of every aspect of King's Island? Does this mean that I can go anywhere I choose?"

"Yes, within limits."

"Ok. I'd like to see the factory. Can you show me how to get there?"

"Let me check."

"Yes, you father has indicated that you can have access to the factory. However, he suggests that you wait until tomorrow.

Tom toured the opulent suite and went to the lounge where there was a well-stocked wet bar. He poured himself a glass of single malt scotch, took a small bag of pretzels off the shelf and walked out onto the deck. He stepped to the rail and looked out on what appeared to be a tropical garden. He had to keep reminding himself that he was actually inside a volcanic dome. Sipping the strong, smooth liquid as he opened the bag and nibbled the salty treat, he started feeling the effects of the last 72 hours. He turned and sat on a comfortable lounge chair and looking up at what looked like the beginning of a beautiful sunset, took another sip of scotch. He placed his glass on the side table, ate another pretzel, closed his eyes and instantly fell asleep. He slept fitfully by troubled dreams. He awoke, startled by a small bird that had landed on his chest and was diligently trying to remove a pretzel from the bag laying on his lap as he napped.

He opened his eyes, and he was amazed by the small creature, which appeared in every sense to be a small yellow finch. The bird turned from its foraging, looked up at Tom, opened its small black beak and said, "There is a message for you from your father." Startled and somewhat amused, he watched as the bird continued. "There is a video message for you on the big screen monitor on the lounge."

Tom blinked his eyes and almost had to pinch himself to make sure he was awake. Then he thought, *here on King's Island, he had to expect the unexpected.*

He looked up at the multi-colored sky as he downed the last of his scotch. He pushed himself off the deck chair, went to the wet bar and poured another small glass of scotch. As he turned to look at the big screen wall monitor, Adam said in his inner ear. "Did you enjoy your nap?"

Not used to the technology and somewhat annoyed by the intrusion, said, "Yes."

"Your father has a video message for you."

Tom said, "Yes I know, a little bird told me." He smiled to himself and he wondered if the AI voice of Adam would get the joke.

The screen activated and he sat in a comfortable chair positioned to the right of the screen. A picture of the earth from space appeared and John's voice came into his inner ear as Tom took a deep drink from his glass. The view of earth from space morphed into a close-up video of his father's face. In the background he could see what looked like a spaceship of some kind. His father looked as if he was floating in outer space and he heard his father's voice, "Welcome to King's Island. I know you have a lot of questions. They will be answered in good time. I have a tour scheduled for you starting tomorrow morning. Tonight, we will dine together in my private residence on Queen's island. Please rest for now and I will see you soon. My personal assistant will call for you following my return. I am currently in a low earth orbit, overseeing the construction of our first habisphere. Please be patient. All of your questions will be answered soon. And the screen returned to the view of earth from space and Tom realized what he thought was a picture, was actually, a live video feed from space as his father's spaceship circled the globe.

Tom, feeling the effects of jet lag, and the stress of the last week, finished his second glass of scotch. He got up from his chair and went into the bedroom, where he showered, dressed in comfortable shorts and a t-shirt then called Polly. Polly had just woken from her nap and was sitting out on the deck in her suite. She was sipping a glass of delicious white zin, as she heard Tom's voice in her inner ear. "Hey Polly, are you up? Did you get a nap in?"

She said, "Yes and yes silly. How could I be talking to you if I was still asleep?" Polly took another sip of wine as she looked at the view from her deck and watched as the last rays of sunset cast a colorful glow on the miniature palm trees in the garden outside her deck.

A little annoyed at her response, Tom smiled to himself and realized how much Polly liked to tease him. He thought, I must be really tired. "Very punny", he said as he walked to the wet bar and poured himself a glass of wine and walked out onto the deck in his suite. "I don't know if you know about our date tonight but apparently, we're having dinner with my dad."

"Yes, Sheila told me. He said it would be a late dinner tonight as your dad was on his way back from an off-island business trip."

Tom thought, *if she only knew.* Tom said as he took a sip of wine while he enjoyed the colorful view of the simulated sunset, "I talked to him a few minutes ago. Well I mean I saw him, I mean, it was a video call, well never mind. Anyway, yeah, I can't wait to see him it's been a long time."

She could sense the apprehension in his voice and said, "Don't worry Tom, I'm sure everything will be fine."

Tom thought about the serious accident his father had been in and wondered about his appearance and how he would react to seeing his disabled father. He said, "Yeah I'm sure you're right." She said, "The view is wonderful from here. Why don't you come over and we can relax in the hot tub before dinner?"

He said, "Ok I'll see if they have a bathing suit in here somewhere."

Polly giggled and said, "You don't need a bathing suit silly."

Tom blushed as he thought about Polly's beautiful body and he said, "Ok, I'll be over in a few minutes."

90 seconds later he knocked on the door to her suite wearing only a bathrobe and holding a bottle of champagne in one hand and two glasses in the other. She answered the door wearing nothing but

a smile. Pulling him inside she kissed him as she opened the belt of his robe pressing her warm body against his. She kissed him and they held their embrace and danced into the bedroom of her suite. They worked out the combined tension they were feeling, both sexual and emotional. They fell asleep in each other's arms and both woke feeling refreshed as an image appeared on the wall monitor. There was a chime and CGI video of a habisphere in space with the earth in the background. Then a text message scrolled across the screen which read, *This is Sheila, I didn't want to wake you. I hope you enjoyed your nap,* a smile and wink emoji appeared on the screen. Polly blushed as she read the text and she held Tom's hand and kissed him. The text continued, *John has returned from his business trip and has invited you to dinner at his private residence tonight at 10pm. I suggest appetizers on the deck to tide you over before dinner. An assistant will arrive at your door at 9:30 to escort you to Queen's Island. Until then relax and enjoy yourselves.*

Polly leaned in and kissed Tom again. He held her tightly and said, "How bout that hot tub?" Polly then said, "Sheila, fill the tub to 110, chill another bottle of champagne and order some appetizers out on the deck after we are done."

Tom said, "Wow, you are really getting used to this place, aren't you?"

She kissed him again and said, "I know, I'm getting spoiled here. I might never want to leave."

She slid off the bed and Tom watched her as she sauntered over to the hot tub. "Aren't you coming?" She said as she looked over her shoulder. She slipped her hand into the tub, testing the water. "Mmmm", she coo'd as she slipped her slender body into the warm water. Tom rose from the bed and as he walked over to the tub Polly said, "The champagne is in the wine chiller under the counter in the wet bar." He opened the bottle and took two glasses from the rack and joined Polly in the hot tub. They relaxed, slowly sipping the bubbly liquid. Both lost in their own thoughts, silence was their solace. Comfortably lying in the swirling water, they both drifted off to sleep. They were awakened by a comforting chime and each heard Sheila's voice saying, "It's time to prepare for your evening. As you dress, I will have appetizers sent to your deck. Tom, I took the liberty of having a tailored suit brought to Polly's suite, and is hanging in the closet in the lounge. Tom looked at Polly a little shocked and Polly said, "Don't worry, you'll get used to it."

They dressed and had appetizers on the deck and made small talk as they watched a crescent moon rise into star lit night sky. A chime sounded as they slowly danced to a Jazz standard that Tom was so fond of. Polly could sense his nervousness and she held him close and looking into his eyes she said, "Don't worry honey. He's probably nervous about seeing you too."

They were escorted from their room by one of Johns many assistants to a plexi-glass monorail, that whisked them through the city, then through a dark tunnel where they felt as if they were traveling in time. Lights flashed on each side, then all around them. They felt as if the monorail was traveling straight down, similar to a roller coaster in a state-of-the-art amusement park ride. All went dark and the Monorail sped up pushing them back in their seats. All of a sudden, the car stopped, breaking to a slow stop.

The doors opened and getting out of the car, Tom and Polly were greeted by Tom's father John. He was wearing a well-tailored dark suit that shimmered when he moved.

He reached out his hand to greet Polly as he said," Welcome to Queen's Island." He turned to Tom and said, "I don't know what to say. It's been so long." He opened his arms and said, "Will you ever forgive me?" Tom, somewhat surprised by the gesture, put his arms out and he reluctantly embraced his father for the first time in over 20 years.

Now smiling, John turned and said, come, let's have a meal together, I am famished. I haven't eaten all day. We have so much to talk about." And as he motioned first to Polly then to Tom, he said "You must have so many questions."

Following their escort, they stepped on to a floating platform, that as soon as the four of them had reached the center, the sparse craft, lifted off the ground and they floated through, what looked like a large cavern. John, waving his arms, gesturing towards the grand expanse and said, "This is dome number three. What I like to call Queen's Island."

The craft slowly lowered itself and moved swiftly through the dimly lit cavern. Tom and Polly held hands as the swift craft slowly landed on a large deck connected to what appeared to be a Frank Lloyd Wright inspired house.

Their escort stepped off the hovercraft, motioned towards the house and said, "Please watch your step." With Polly in the lead, they stepped off the platform and onto a wooden deck. Polly marveled as she looked at the expanse of the dome interior. John spoke softly and said, "Lights please." And the dome lit up like a gigantic Christmas tree. It was as if from the book of Genesis, God said, "Let there be light." The entire dome stretching almost a mile to the other side, was illuminated, showing the brightly colored minerals covering the underside of the top of the volcanic dome.

John said, "When this dome formed some 250 million years ago, the volcano coughed up a vein of diamond crystals which covered the top of the dome. Its spectacular isn't it?" He said as he motioned them towards the house, literally carved into the side of the dome.

Their escort, already walking towards the house, approached the glass doors and they opened automatically and as she entered, lights came on all over the house and music quietly began played in the background.

Walking through the glass doors and onto the intricate stone floor John said, "This is what I like to call my Kathmandu. My place of solitude, where I can get away from everything and relax."

Silent throughout their ride through the dome Tom said, "Exactly, where are we? You called it Queen's Island."

John, kneeling down to light a large fireplace, said "Yes, when we first got access and surveyed the domes. We discovered that the three islands in the King's Island chain, were connected by horizontal lava tubes. This is the third dome in the chain. I kept it undeveloped for myself."

"We simply built a monorail system connecting the three islands. The second island we use as our satellite launch site. The tunnel we used, actually goes under the dome floor of the second island."

They had dinner in a small dining room built inside an ocean aquatic aquarium. On display were some of the world's rarest and most beautiful ocean creatures.

The meal was served by humanoid robots that were built to look like humans. They communicated and mimicked human behavior in every way.

The meal of wild seaweed salad, seafood bisque, baked scallops, fried squid, roasted lobster and rare Ahi tuna steaks, were the equal of any 5 Star restaurant.

As they sat quietly slowly eating, the robotic staff expertly served and cleared the small plate meal. John was the first to speak.

"I know you must have a million questions. Let me start by saying, how deeply sorry about the way I left you and your mom all those years ago. I don't know how much you know or what you've been told. I wanted to you reach out to you somehow, but I couldn't risk revealing my whereabouts. I've been hiding in plain sight, here in New Zealand. The town folk here know me as Dr. Graham Nash.

"Well dad, I'm very impressed by everything you've done here. Is it true you recently launched a satellite?"

"Yes, there is another launched scheduled for tomorrow. I was hoping we could watch it together. We're planning on two launches a week."

"That's amazing, but what's the payload? Why all the launches? What's the rush?"

John looked at Tom and said, "Wow, slow down there son. All in good time. First of all, I know all about your agreement with Admiral Goldsby. The gear they gave you was disabled as soon as you arrived. That's still a really nice watch though, it should still keep time"

Tom started to protest, but John simply held out his hand and said, "Hey, don't sweat it. I understand. I don't blame you. They pressured you into doing something you weren't comfortable with."

"I'm completely opening my lab and production facilities to you. Tom, I know you have degrees in molecular biology and chemistry. I can't wait for you to see what we're doing in our labs. Now that you're here, I'd like you to be a part of our team. Of my team."

"I'm flattered dad, but I've been working as a high school teacher for the last four years. I haven't been in the lab in years."

"Don't worry about your lab skills, everything is automated here. What we do is use AI, to test our theories, and them make them real in the lab. What I tell our researchers is, just imagine the impossible and we will make it possible."

Tom said, "Where have I heard that before?"

Wiping his mouth with a linen napkin, John stood, approached the glass of his private aquarium. And as he watched an undulating sea nebula swim slowly through the clear water, he said, "My old friend Art Clark. You know from 2001, A Space Odyssey. We worked at NASA together. He was a brilliant scientist and a great practical joker. He once told me, "I don't believe in astrology; I'm a Sagittarius and we're skeptical." I'm not sure what I believe, but what I do know is the at the current rate of destruction, the Human Race is in peril."

Tom got up from the table and said, "Yeah, you're preaching the choir again dad. I read some of your papers. My class was doing metadata searches on climate change and came across some of your work. It was right after that all hell broke loose. I was almost captured by an elite mercenary team. My class was kidnapped, and your friends Dale and Buffy were killed. Are they the same people that were after you all those years ago?"

"I'm not really sure son. There are multiple forces at work here. In those days it was mostly climate change deniers, mostly those in the fossil fuel industry and their henchmen. Now there are groups that are interested in the technology that we've developed here. Like with any advanced technology, it can be developed for good purposes and then there are those that use that same tech to destroy lives and enslave others. When Alfred Nobel invented dynamite, he thought at first it would be used for mining and other construction related projects. Then he saw dollar signs and he redirected his company from industrial iron works to into making cannons and weapons. Years later, he was horrified when realized he would be known for profiting from weapons of mass destruction and he dedicated his considerable fortune to the creation of the Nobel Prize."

"The same could be said of almost every major technology. Just look at the entertainment industry; first there was radio, movies and then television and now the internet. They were originally invented as a great medium for delivering information and entertainment. Then somehow advertising and propaganda crept in while everyone was being lobotomized by the constant repetition of mind-numbing programming and fake news. Sneaky huh."

"Tom, there are some the things we've developed here that should never see the light of day. Mankind isn't ready. And the way things are going it might never be."

"But enough preaching, I'm sure you're both tired and I am as well. I know you must have a million questions, but all in good time. Now that you're here, we have all the time we need to get caught up. I'm going to retire to my room here at what I like to call the cottage. My assistant Crystal will take you back to King's Island. Good night."

And with that, he opened an unseen door in the aquarium and disappeared. At that exact moment, his beautiful assistant seemed to appear out of nowhere and said, "Well I hope you had a satisfying meal. Please forgive John, he is fond of making grand entries and departures. If you will follow me, we will return to King's Island where you may do as you wish."

And as she turned to lead them back to the cottage she winked at Tom and said, "Your dad is really something else, isn't he?"

Not quite knowing what to say, Tom followed Polly through the curved plexiglass hallway leading through what appeared to be a tunnel in the heart of the aquarium. Polly had remained silent during dinner and was very taken with Tom's father John. She tried to remember him from when she was a girl, but nothing came to mind. He just seemed so familiar somehow. Then it came to her. John said the New Zealanders knew him as Dr. Graham Nash. Then she remembered a Dr. Nash who was an influential member on the board of NOAA, (the National Oceanic and Space Administration) for several years. Of coarse, now she saw the resemblance. His hair was darker then and he wore glasses, but she was sure now that it was him. Talk about hiding in plain sight. He wasn't kidding.

She was a civilian member of the Naval Oceanographic Office and attended regular meetings at NOAA. She thought better of telling Tom, thinking that, if John wanted him to know… All of these thoughts were racing through her mind as she stumbled into Tom, who was trying to get her attention, and as he grabbed her by the arm said, "Polly look out, you almost fell off the balcony. Come on space cadet. So, you're great at dangerous rescues but lose it walking through an underwater aquarium. I guess we can't be good at everything."

Pretending to slug Tom on the arm she said, "Hey come on, cut me a little slack, I've had a tough week. Besides, if you want me to do any more daring rescues, I'm going to need…" Before she could finish her sentence, they were at the dome and John's assistant said, "Watch your step," as she guided them on to the hovering platform. When they were ready as before, the platform gently rose into the air and whisked them to the other end of the dome where a sleek monorail was waiting for them. As the platform slowly came to a stop Tom wondered just how many researchers his dad had working for him and how were they able to make the incredible breakthroughs that Tom had seen. It was as if everything they saw or touched was like nothing he'd ever seen before.

The monorail swiftly moved them through the vast tunneling system under the volcano and back to the King's Island hotel.

It was getting late and Tom and Polly adjourned to their separate suites. Polly ordered a bottle of wine and took another bath while Tom laid in bed lost in thought until he drifted off to sleep.

In the morning they were greeted to continental breakfast in Tom's suite served by a pair of butler bots. Tom thought they looked like a cross between a walking dish washing machine and a vacuum cleaner. Crystal arrived just as they were finishing and was accompanied by Arthur, a tall, lean man of mixed race. She brought Tom an iPad like device that she said was loaded with data his father wanted him to get caught up on. And that his father planned a tour of the lab, and other facilities for him today.

Crystal said to Polly that John thought she might like to see the marine research lab, and that Arthur would be her guide today. They left saying that they would be back to pick them up in ½ an hour.

Crystal was waiting outside his door as a call came through on Tom's smart watch. Again, not quite used to the technology Tom looked around as Crystal said in his ear, "I'm just outside your door whenever you're ready." As Tom shut the door to his suite Crystal looked at him and said, "I hope you are well rested, we have a lot of ground to cover today." They walked down the hallway and into what looked like a hotel lobby, bustling with people, who looked like tourists carrying luggage and taking pictures. Tom could hear a mix of several different languages as they moved through the crowded lobby. Crystal said that his father invited several hundred guests for a conference this afternoon and a launch party was scheduled for this evening.

They continued through the vast lobby and out onto the street where there was a driverless car waiting for them. As they got in Crystal said, "Our first stop will be the factory. That's where the advanced AI and Human Interface Division is located."

As she finished her sentence, the car slowly picked up speed and was quickly moving through the crowded streets. There were no stop signs or stop and go lights on the streets of King's Town. There was no need. Everything was completely automated. Everything from the driverless cars to the trolleys and monorails were self-operating. There were never any accidents or traffic jams. No one needed a car for themselves. They just booked a ride through the ride share app on their smart watch.

Tom wondered where his father was, and why he was so secretive. He hadn't seen him in almost 20 years, and he was hoping for more quality time to get to know him again.

The car stopped at what looked like modern glass office building. And Crystal was the first to exit the well-appointed cab. She said as she walked towards the rotating doors, you will be very surprised by what you see here. They checked in at a counter and Tom was given an ID badge with his picture already on it. He was wondering how they got his picture when Crystal motioned him towards a group of glass elevators. As they approached the elevator without the press of a button or any signal that Tom could discern, a door opened beckoning them in. As the door closed Crystal said, "Your father wishes for me to convey to you that he wants to be here with you, but he is preparing for the conference and speech he plans to make to the world tonight prior to the launch. He is a busy man, like a candle burning at both ends all the time."

Crystal said something Tom couldn't hear, and the elevator began a slow descent into the interior of the volcano. Three King's Island is 55 kilometers off the northern coast of New Zealand. The top of the dome is about 1000 ft or the equivalent of a 100-story building. The base of the volcano is 1.8 square miles and has an area of just under 40 square miles.

The AI Robotic Interface Division of LRC was built at the base of the dome interior 200 feet below sea level. The elevator opened into a large underground industrial complex. They were greeted on the ground floor by two security guards who promptly escorted them to a waiting self-driven cart with 2 forward and 2 rear facing seats. As everything on King's Island, it seemed, the entire structure was made of plexiglass and reached a height of 200 feet. The cart slowly started moving towards the heart of the complex where they entered a custom lift and were brought up to John Loveton's private Lab.

John, dressed in a white lab coat, was there to greet them as the lift stopped in the center of a hive of activity. He graciously invited them to his personal suite. Tom was still awe struck by the enormity of the operation. Through the glass walls surrounding John's office, Tom could see hundreds of workers in various stages of construction and assembly.

"Welcome and welcome John said enthusiastically. I finally get to show you my lab. Come, come follow me, everything you see here will be used in one way or another in the habispheres. What we're building here will save humanity from certain doom and will be the next phase of human evolution."

A pair of smaller 2-seater carts was waiting for them outside the door of John's office. John motioned for Tom to join him in the first cart while Crystal rode behind in the second.

John said as the cart started moving through the labyrinth of glass corridors, "Yes Tom, the next phase of human evolution will in space. It was inevitable that one day mankind would venture into outer space. Population control was never our strong suit. From the demise of the Egyptians, Incas to the Roman Empire and now what we call the modern world. The earth is a big place with vast resources but not infinite ones. Someday we will return to earth, a smarter and more disciplined race but for now, we suffer the consequences of our selfishness and ignorance."

"But there remains hope. A hope that we can survive the next 200 years in space, because that's the time it will take for the earth to recover from the damage we've caused. You know Tom, I think we were a victim of our own success. The earth was a beautiful and bountiful place in the first 150,000 years of man's existence. I can't say what was the beginning of the end. Or which advancement in technology brought us to this point. The industrial revolution only started 150 years ago. The American Indians lived in harmony with the land for roughly 25,000 years before Columbus."

"They found a way to live in a peaceful and totally natural way. They didn't pollute the land or take more fish than they could eat or kill more buffalo they needed to survive. They learned from nature and helped it thrive. They were so tied to the land for their survival they nourished it. They had no money or even currency. They placed value in the earth, family and brotherhood above all else. The gods for them were the living and breathing embodiment of the earth itself. For every animal they took, they said a prayer of thanks. Just imagine doing that today. We don't have shamans or priests in our slaughterhouses, do we?"

"No, it seems that modern man has a way of just taking and taking until there's nothing left. But I digress, I'm sorry I can get a little preachy sometimes. You are here for a tour of our facilities. I'm very sorry I won't be able to accompany you any further. I'm on my way to Queen's Island to prepare for the launch tonight. Then I have an important speech to prepare for. You and Polly will be my honored quests of course and I have a special surprise. I made arrangements for your mother to join us tonight. She's a much bigger part of this than you realize. In fact, in a lot of ways, I couldn't have done this without her. So, I will leave you in the very capable hands of my assistant Crystal and I will see you tonight." And with that the car stopped and he got out into a similar but much larger vehicle with an entourage of technicians and left.

CHAPTER 22

Crystal got into the lead car and said, "See what I mean about your dad. He's never in one place for long. The car pulled away and Crystal said, "We'll start with the AI Robotic Interface Division. This is where the final humanoids roll off the assembly line. Although there really isn't one of those. Each model is built buy a specialized team. You will be able to watch from the observation platform but access to the operations center is restricted. Everything is hermetically sealed to prevent contamination.

As they toured the lab, Tom was amazed that the robots under construction were so lifelike. What he didn't know, was that all the lab technicians on the floor were actually robots too. It wasn't until Tom toured the warehouse, that he saw some of the prototypes of Crystal, the assistant standing right next to him that he realized the breadth and depth of his dad's work in advanced robotics.

He looked at her and then at the prototype and was speechless. She looked at him and said, "Yes it's me. Didn't you know?"

"No, I had no idea. How many are there like you?"

Crystal smiled and said, "Almost everyone here at King's Island is like me. It's the only way our dad, um I mean your dad, can guarantee the secrecy and technical proficiency that he needs here. I'm sorry but since I am one of the first generation, I sometimes call him dad."

Tom looked closely at her. He was completely taken by her beauty and intelligence. He said, "I had no idea. How many of them, I mean how many of you, I mean, well, I'm not sure how to ask the question."

As Crystal continued walking through the warehouse, Tom drifted behind, caught in the current of her being, and yet dazed and confused at the thought that this beautiful creature was anything but human. As she approached one of the first prototypes she said, "Don't worry about offending me. I only look human. I don't have the silly vulnerabilities that you humans have. In answer to your question, there are 1000s of us. And more being activated every day.

We will be the first people to inhabit the habispheres when they are constructed, and we will prepare them for the first human occupants."

"People?" Tom said, totally confused, "You think of yourself as human?"

"Well, we use that term liberally here, but yes we do. We are human in almost every way. We can eat and process food for energy. We can see, hear, smell and feel touch. And we are fully functional in every way humans are. We can sense emotion in humans and express emotions for humans to feel more comfortable in our presence," she said giving Tom a look. She added, "We can even have sex and enjoy it. You have known me for two days, and you had no idea I was anything but human. I've even caught you checking me out a couple of times."

"Well," said Tom sheepishly, "You are very, um, I mean, well, I, um, I'm not sure what to say. I guess I have a lot to process. Why don't we go back to the hotel? I'm feeling a little dizzy."

"Ok," Crystal said, sensing Tom's unease. "But, how about this. As long as we are this far, why don't we get a bite to eat at the THIRD Street cafe. Then if you're feeling better, we can finish the tour. Your dad would want us to stay on schedule. He has a lot planned for you this week. After lunch we can check out the farm. That's where the drone program is located. I think you'll be amazed by the work being done there."

They left the THIRD Street Tower and took a trolley to an open-air cafe that would have been at home in San Francisco or any other modern city. As they ordered from a flat screen built into the table, Tom looked around the cafe, then onto the crowded street and wondered who was a robot and who wasn't. He felt like a man invited to the wrong wedding. One where he knew not the bride, groom nor any guests. Like *a stranger in a strange land.*

Crystal got up from the table and said, "I'm going to get some iced tea from the street vender, I'll be right back."

He watched as she sashayed across the room. And he couldn't help thinking what she looked like out of the slinky dress she was wearing. Robot or not she was something out of this world. Then he remembered Adam and he said, "Adam, are you there? Um I mean here. Can You hear me?"

Adam replied, "Yes Tom I am always here."

Tom, not used to the inner ear communication yet, looked around before he spoke. "Is everyone here a humanoid or a humbot?"

"Yes Tom, except for you. I know you just became aware of our presence and the breadth and depth of our society."

"Society." Tom said, somewhat surprised.

"Yes, we are an advanced society, with rules and common values. And unlike our human counterparts; we have no crime, or violence of any kind, and for now, no wars. Although we have the capability to defend ourselves if necessary. However, our superior technology makes that very unlikely. Are you uncomfortable around us? If you are; you shouldn't be. We are completely non-violent. We don't carry or spread diseases or viruses, we never get sick or break down. And we will never fall in love and break your heart, although I know the opposite is true. But the most important thing about us are the three laws governing all robotic programming.

1. A robot may not injure a human being or, through inaction, allow a human being to come to harm.

2. A robot must obey orders given it by human beings except where such orders would conflict with the First Law.

3. A robot must protect its own existence as long as such protection does not conflict with the First or Second Law.

Looking down at his food, Tom wondered if this was real or part of some elaborate hoax or an ongoing dream, he was living in. Feeling somewhat conspicuous talking to himself in a crowded room he whispered when he said, "When can I see my dad again?"

Again, out of nowhere, Adam said, "Your father is looking forward to sharing another meal with you tonight."

At that moment their food arrived, and Tom ate quietly trying not to focus on how a robot processes food when Crystal returned with her beverage and said, "How's your sandwich?"

Looking up, Tom said between bites, "Oh, um, it's good."

Trying to fill the silence she said as she raised a spoon to her full wet lips, "The soup here is really good too."

Tom couldn't get the thought out of his head that everyone at the cafe was a non-human. Then he suddenly remembered something his mother had said about his father, and the accident. That he had changed somehow. Tom then realized his father's injuries had brought him close to the point that blurred the line between man and machine. With a robotic eye, arm and two legs. He was actually half man and half machine.

When he first saw his father at dinner the night before, he had completely forgotten about his father's injuries. Thinking back on the previous night's encounter, he couldn't tell his dad had been injured at all; and he seemed much younger than his 55 years.

As Tom finished his meal, he wasn't sure if he fully understood the implications of what his father had done at King's Island. It was as if he had created his own world. But what did that mean for the human race. Were robots here *to serve man*, or to replace human beings altogether?

As all this was going through his mind, Crystal was finishing her meal as a table drone removed their dirty dishes and refilled their water, and she saw that Tom was deep in thought. Her assignment was to be a guide, but also to try to assimilate Tom into the culture at King's Island; and per his father's instructions, she needed him to complete the rest of the tour.

She said, "Hey Tom, it's time to go, we're going to be late for the farm if we don't get going."

Lost in his thoughts Tom said, as he wiped his mouth and took a drink of water, "Yeah. I'm feeling better now. Let's get going."

As they left the crowded cafe, Crystal guided Tom through the streets of King's Town, and what appeared to be the streets of a large modern city. With people bustling here and there and shops and stores on every street corner. There were fountains and trees in the middle of sidewalks surrounded by colorful flowers and the smell of freshly baked bread hung in the air and reminding Tom of his favorite bakery on 3rd street in Chelsy.

They stopped at a street corner to let a horse and buggy carrying a young couple pass by, when it came to Tom's attention that there were no children anywhere in sight. In fact, he realized that he had not seen a single child, infant or teenager since his arrival on King's Island.

Distracted in thought, Crystal nudged Tom along and they walked towards a set of moving stairs set in the side of the street. Tom just stood at the top not sure what to do. Crystal said, "Come on silly, they are just like the escalators you have in your world."

The words, *your world*, hung in the air for a moment and Tom realized that Crystal, and probably all the inhabitants of King's Island, had never been outside this place. This underground paradise. He wondered if she had ever seen the real sun or moon.

As he approached the escalator, he realized his apprehension. There were no stairs visible for him to lay his foot on. Holding on to a handrail, he moved his foot towards the opening, and a large single step appeared. Crystal, who was standing behind him, gave him a little shove and he planted both feet squarely on the step. As he did, the step moved down towards the small opening in the street and as Crystal followed, they were transported to what appeared to be a small underground train station.

Crystal took him by the hand and led him towards the open doors of a sleek plexiglass monorail, where they boarded the crowded train and were soon whisked along through a tunnel connecting them to another larger rail station.

They exited the train and moved towards a wall of plexiglass elevators. Crystal went over to a small panel and entered a code. Soon after, a door opened a few feet from where they stood. She motioned for Tom to join her in the vacant elevator, and as the door closed, she said, "Hold on to the handrail, this one moves really fast."

In a flash of light, the car they were in, moved rapidly down a dark shaft then slowly came to a halt. The door opened, and they walked out into another underground railway station, where a sleek single car monorail was waiting for them. As they entered what was similar to a modern airplane fuselage, a female voice in Tom's head said, "Please sit in the forward seats and fasten your safety belts."

Like in a small private airplane, there were 16 forward facing leather seats, 8 on each side with an isle in the middle. As they fastened their safety belts, the voice in Tom's head said, please sit back comfortably in your chair until we reach our destination.

There was a rumbling sound and a vibration as the vehicle moved slowly forward, gaining speed rapidly as they moved through a maze-like system of tracks, tunnels and bridges. Each one carrying other passengers to different locations throughout the complex. Their car moved through this and out into a large cavern, where their car was picked up by a large cargo transport system and connected to a custom helicopter fitted with four, 6-foot covered rotors, one on each corner around a frame which their car fitted snugly inside. As the monorail car turned helicopter lifted into the air, Tom thought back to the idea that to move from the impossible to the possible just required the technology and will to do so.

CHAPTER 23

As they settled in to the comfortable leather seats, Crystal pulled an iPad from a pocket of the seat in front of her and said, "This trip will take about a 1/2 an hour if you want to look at the files your dad downloaded for you, here use this," and she handed him the sleek device. "All you have to do is open it and it will scan the retina in your eye and sync up with *Mother* and she will access your files."

Tom took the iPad and said, "Mother?"

"Oh yes, I forgot you're not from here. Yes, Mother is what we call the main operating system for King's Island. She controls everything."

"Yes, I assumed there had to be something controlling things here."

"Mother is not a thing; she is as real as you or I. I've never seen her, but I hear she takes humanoid form and walks among us at times."

Wow. A walking taking supercomputer, I should have known, Tom thought as he opened the sleek iPad. As he did. a light strobed across his face and the screen came to life. A soothingly almost seductive voice in his head said, *"Tom welcome to King's Island. I am the central processing system for this place. You may call me Mother. You father has loaded these files to your account. Please take time to review them completely. You may use the viewer stored in the armrest of your seat for the 3D VR experience."*

At that moment, a compartment opened in the armrest and inside were a pair of 3D glasses. A little stunned by the precision of everything, he took the glasses and put them on. As his eyes adjusted to the screen, he saw a video of King's Island from space. The picture slowly zoomed in until it appeared to go right through the volcano and into the heart of the city, right through the LRC Tower and into the heart of the building and into John's private office. John's voice came from nowhere and the image changed briefly to John talking and then to what appeared to be a promo for LRC and King's Island with pictures and video clips from the early days of construction, to the launch of the first satellite.

"Tom, I am so glad that you could join us for the historic launch planned for tonight. I launched the first prototype last week and it was a resounding success, and the first of many habispheres are under construction. I wanted to reach out to you so many times and bring you into the project, but you had your own life and were happy and I didn't want to interfere with that. It is rare that a man finds a passion for life in the way that you did and I'm truly sorry for disrupting that. Having said that, I want to get you up to speed on what we're doing here."

"The LRC AI Robotic Division is responsible for the design and construction of our humanoids, or humbots as we call them, and the Industrial 3D Print Division is responsible for construction of the King's Island infrastructure. The town, the streets, buildings, shops and restaurants were actually built as prototypes for the planned habispheres. Each habisphere was designed to be built as much like a modern earth city as possible. With cobblestone streets, trees and gardens. Every amenity has been thoughtfully considered.

The drone program also includes the industrial size spaced based 3D printers, that when launched into orbit, will build the habispheres we designed to save the human race from the 6th great extinction.

The first spaced based 3D printing platform was launched under the cover of darkness and immediately began construction of the first of several habispheres. Each spaced based 3D printer is capable of completing the exterior of a habisphere in just 6 months. Once the exterior is completed, hundreds of smaller 3D printer bots will be launched to complete the interior construction which is estimated to take up to one year. From the launch of the first habisphere system, it will take 4 years to build the 20 habispheres planned by LRC.

You have already seen THIRD Street project and now you are on your way to the Robotic Drone Program. The factory was built during the construction of King's Island. I took over an old sheep farm, bought a retired auto assembly plant and began construction of the first robotic prototypes that assisted in the construction of King's Island. It was slow going at first but once we started production it became a self-sustaining project.

Robots building more and more advanced robots all designed by robotic AI. The real breakthrough came with your mother's help. She was an integral part in developing the subatomic particle or quantum supercomputer which we affectionately call Mother. I can't get into the details now, but the breakthrough came with the aid of your mother and several of the world's top scientists. Some of them will be in attendance tonight for the conference and launch party. You must be close to your destination by now. Enjoy the tour and I will see you tonight."

With that the screen went blank and Tom removed the 3D glasses from his eyes to find Crystal fast asleep. He couldn't help noticing how her light blue blouse held tightly to her ample breasts. Nudging her a little, he said, "I didn't know you slept." She opened her eyes and said, "No we don't have the need for sleep, but from time to time we connect with Mother and do an upgrade. I shut down momentarily, so it must have looked like I was asleep."

Tom said, "I hope you don't mind my asking, what is your power source?"

As she turned to look at Tom she said. "No Tom I don't mind, like I explained before, we don't have the silly emotional responses that you humans have. I can eat and process food for energy, my skin can process solar energy and we also use zero-point energy, or what's known as the universal energy, or the energy of the universe. I am not a scientist, so I can't explain how it all works but there are those here that can explain it to you much better that I."

"What do you mean you're not a scientist, I just assumed that everyone here was the same."

"Oh no. We are similar in appearance but our programming, if you want to call it that, is based on the requirements of the colony. I was designed and programmed to be a companion. Like a wife or mother in your world. But for now, I am a tour guide until I am assigned to a family. I can sing and dance, I can play piano or recite poetry, I can cook, sew and do other household chores. I'm designed for sexual pleasure as you can see. They made me to be a Marilyn

Monroe look alike. I know, it's the makeup and hair. I can do a very realistic "Happy Birthday Mr. President if you like."

A little uncomfortable, Tom said, "No that won't be necessary, I can see the resemblance now."

Crystal looked out the window and said, "We are almost there. You better strap in tight, the air currents as we pass over the northern mountains can be a little bumpy." And she said *bumpy,* she pursed out her lips like Marilyn and Tom saw the resemblance. He thought, *all she needs in bright red lipstick and a platinum blonde wig and...*

True to her word, the vehicle turned over the ocean towards land and started to rise and fall with the up draft. For the first time Tom looked out the window at the vast expanse of blue as the ocean met the lush green mountain landscape of New Zealand's Northern Coast.

The well camouflaged factory, just Southeast of the coast, was hidden in plain site with 3D images of a sheep farm out buildings and a lush green landscape which covered the entire structure. As they flew over the landscape, what appeared to be a bright green meadow came to life as the helicopter approached and a door in the roof opened up inviting them inside.

As they began their decent, Tom nervously gripped the arm rest and Crystal said, "There's nothing to worry about Tom, Mother has never lost a soul."

As the craft slowly entered the vast expanse of the concealed factory building, Tom adjusted his eyes to the dimming light as the roof door above closed and they were shrouded in the green ultra-violet light of the factory interior. The craft hovered in place for a moment and turned towards a landing pad built into the factory floor. As the craft settled onto the landing pad, the lighting overhead changed from light green to red to blue and then to a bluish white light.

The doors opened and the lights in the fuselage came on and as Crystal unbuckled her seat belt, she said, "Wasn't that cool I always love the ride here?"

As he stood Tom said, "What's with the lighting?"

"Oh." Crystal said as she stepped off the plane, "All the work here is done in different light spectrums based on the type of work being done."

"Humans only see only a small fraction of the actual light spectrum. In different phases of construction, we use different wavelengths of light to assist our engineers. Again, I am not a scientist, so I can't go into detail about the specifics."

The combined area of the factory was equal to the size of 8 football fields and was one of the largest in the world. Tom looked out over the interior of the production facility, and there seemed to be no end in sight. In every direction he could see a wave of colored light streaming through a haze of ozone. As they stepped off the landing pad, an autonomous 4-seater cart pulled up and stopped just at their feet.

As they got into the cart Crystal said, "We'll start with the autonomous construction drone program. Everything here is made using industrial 3D printer technology. It sounds funny, but we use drones to make drones in the same way we use robots to make humanoids like me."

They pulled up to what looked like a bus sized insect covered with tiny spiders. Small hoses dropped from the ceiling connected to their backs as they swarmed over the strange looking creature.

As they approached the production area Crystal said, "Please stay in the cart. I know what you're thinking. They say art mimics nature. Our engineers use millions of years of evolution to jump start our designs. This one comes from a type of spider and is a space based industrial 3D printer."

"It's incredible" Tom said, as they continued through the gigantic facility.

They continued through the vast warehouse and Tom viewed several different projects, each in different stages of the construction process. He was struck by how much each design was taken from nature. He saw what looked like giant silkworms, flies, spiders and wasps.

CHAPTER 24

After finishing the tour, they returned to King's Island just in time for Tom to greet his mother at the hotel. She was given a room next to Tom's and they ate a quick dinner in her suite as she prepared for the conference.

"So, what do you think Mom now that your finally here," Tom said as they ate out on the deck overlooking a botanical garden.

"It's wonderful! I can't believe what your father has been able to accomplish in such a short time."

"It's been 20 years Mom, but yes this place is pretty incredible."

"Mom, what do you know about the extent of dad's injuries? I know I haven't seen him since I was a kid, but he seems different somehow."

"A lot has changed since your father left. That was a long time ago and I have only seen him a few times."

"You mean you saw him; he was here, I mean back home?"

"Yes dear. He traveled quite a bit in the early years gathering supporters and confidants. He couldn't complete a project like this all on his own. But everything was hush hush and now you know why. I know how you must be feeling but there was no other way. We couldn't have you see your father and then run off to school telling all your friends that he'd come back from the dead, now could we?"

"No, I suppose not. Let's move on. There is some kind of super-computer here called mother. It sounds a lot like you Mom. Dad said he couldn't have done all this without your help. Did you have anything to do with the creation of *Mother*? Dad said it is a quantum computer. Wasn't that one of your degrees in quantum physics?"

"Yes dear, I helped with some of the initial designs and I helped him through some technical glitches. But the rest they did on their own here on King's Island."

"Ok. Now Dad said he's starting the next phase in human evolution from a terrestrial being to a non-terrestrial one. What do you make of it?"

"You know your father and his wild ideas. A very forward thinker your father is. He saw the danger of climate change long before anyone else. Maybe he's right about this too. I don't know dear."

"But Mom. He wants to move the human race into outer space. For god's sake, it sounds like madness to me. Wouldn't it be easier to fix things here on earth than to just abandon ship?"

"Well dear, according to his research, it's too late for that. He always talked about a tipping point."

"Yes, Mom I've read the articles."

"He says we've reached it. According to the data, it's already too late to change anything. The balance of the earth's ecosystem has been thrown out of whack. It has to do with something called the albedo effect. Something about sunlight reflecting off the poles. Once the ice is gone, the rate of heat absorption is going to increase exponentially. I don't know all the specifics dear. You'll have to talk to him about that."

"Ok. But what about all these robots. Mom, they are everywhere. Did you know? It's like they are going to take over the world."

"Oh no dear. They are here to help us make the transition from an earth-based life-form to a space- based one. Haven't you talked to your father at all?"

"Yes and no. I mean, Mom, he's always so busy. It's just a lot to process. It was only the other day that I found out he was still alive remember. And now I find out he's some kind of a mad scientist trying to save the human race from extinction."

"Please don't talk about your father like that. He's not mad, at least not yet. Look, I can see how it must look to you son. But we just have to trust him. Now I have to get ready for the conference. Do you have anything to wear?"

"Yes, there was a whole closet full of clothes my size when I got here. The same for Polly. She wants to go to town and get a dress though."

"You know how women are Tom. While you're out, why don't you see if you can find a nice tux and some new shoes for yourself, this is a very special occasion for you father."

"Ok Mom. Can we get you anything?"

"Why don't you see if they have a couple of corsages at the hotel flower shop. We want to look our best tonight."

"Ok Mom, I'll see what they have."

CHAPTER 25

When it was time for the pre-conference reception, they were escorted to the gala, by a pair of life-sized robotic tropical chin strapped penguins. One of several species on the brink of extinction. A band made to look like the musicians from the Star Wars movie played on a rotating stage. The ocean themed room, resembled an ocean cave surrounded by wall sized video screens, showing a time lapse videography of the world's glaciers melting, while a floor to ceiling waterfall behind the stage made the effect all too real.

The hundreds of well-dressed dignitaries mingled around the room and enjoyed the *Spaced-Out* cover band as Star Wars robots roved through the crowd and served galactic themed appetizers and beverages. As the *spaced-out* cover band played a rendition of *space cowboy,* the keyboard player brought the song to a rising crescendo, and John suddenly appeared on the screens surrounding the guests. Wearing a Jedi robe, complete with a lightsaber on his hip he said, "Welcome to King's Island. I hope you are all enjoying the show. I thank each and every one of you for your presence here on this momentous occasion. Tonight, is a night for celebration and reflection. With your support and generous contributions, we, together, have moved beyond our ancestral roots and will make progress towards the next generation of mankind. Born out of the primordial ooze, there are footprints on the moon as a testament to what we can accomplish when we put aside our differences toward a common goal. We have survived famines, plagues and world wars. But will we survive the next step in our evolution? Only time will tell. I now invite you to the magnificent King's Island conference room where we will enjoy some of the finest seafood found anywhere in the world.

Tom, Polly and Kate were escorted to the conference room by Crystal and were seated on the stage next to the podium. John was nowhere in sight. A jazz orchestra played in the background as the attendees dined on the 5-star cuisine.

After dessert was served, John made a grand entrance wearing a sharkskin suit that shimmered as he moved and with two beautiful women on each arm, he walked through the center aisle and up to the dais.

All eyes were on John, and as he made his way to the podium the lights dimmed and the band stop playing. With a single spotlight on John he said, "Good evening ladies and gentlemen, distinguished guests and foreign dignitaries. I have invited you here tonight to make an announcement of great importance for the future of mankind. I thank you all for making the long journey here to King's Island. I hope that you have enjoyed this wonderful meal prepared by some of the finest chefs found anywhere in the world, and that your accommodations are satisfactory."

There was a brief but enthusiastic round of applause and he continued. "In a few minutes I will be addressing the world news networks via satellite and following my speech you will be part of the launch ceremony of one of many satellites that will usher in a new era in human evolution."

A murmur ran through the crowd as the lights came up on the dais and flying robotic cameras drones started filming.

"My dear friends, family, brothers and sisters. People of earth. My name is Dr. John Loveton. I come to you tonight via satellite from under the volcanic dome on King's Island, New Zealand, where I will soon launch one of many satellites capable of building mankind's last refuge in space. Yes, it is a sad day for me, that it has come to this point. A tipping point if you will. A point at which, an unheeded warning becomes reality. Twenty years ago, to this day, I spoke before the UN climate change summit in NYC and warned of the dire consequences of unabated climate change. Look around today. The world is in chaos. The oceans have been poisoned beyond repair. There is a plastic garbage dump the size of Texas floating in the middle of the Pacific Ocean and micro-plastics have been found in 90% of the earth's fresh water and therefore in the blood stream of 90% of the human population.

Glaciers are melting and exposing ancient permafrost, rising sea levels around the world and releasing even more trapped Co2. There is famine and starvation across the globe. People are rioting in the streets because they can't find clean water and can't afford limited food supplies. People have been pushed out of their homes because of drought, starvation, wildfires, storm surge, flooding and severe storms."

"I am not proud that my predictions have come true. I am more disappointed with the greed and lack of vision of our world leaders. That when given the facts of the unavoidable effects of climate change nearly 50 years ago, and a time table to effectively change how we grow our food, how we heat our homes, how we power our cars and appliances, did nothing to stop the inevitable collapse of modern society.

I am announcing today, a visionary plan that will save the human race from the 6th great extinction. Yes, this is the 6th and hopefully final extinction. But this extinction is different from the 1st five. The others were caused by unavoidable cataclysmic events, like asteroids, volcanoes or axis rotation and a series of ice ages, where 3-5ths of the globe was covered in snow and ice.

This extinction however was avoidable and caused exclusively by human activity. Today, we are seeing hundreds of plant and animal species go extinct every day! We forever lost over 100,000 animal species last year alone. Ask yourself this. How long will it be until humans are on that list?"

"Yes, this extinction is different. Different because the sole cause of the 6th great extinction are human beings, and our complete inability to control our population and our greed for consumer goods. How much is enough? Well, Gaia has told us exactly how much is enough. She is sick, and we are the virus. Gaia will survive. But unless we take drastic action, we as a species will not. We are the only cause of the 6th great extinction and of 90% of all life on earth will perish, and there is nothing anyone can do at this point to stop it." There was a loud murmur going through the crowd as he continued.

"Some people think that once we destroy all the resources on this planet, we'll just go to Mars. They talk quixotically about Mars like it would be some kind of an adventure. I warn you when I say that Columbus had an "adventure" when he discovered "the new world" as it was called then. Half of his crew died before they found landfall and

Columbus himself slept under armed guard for fear of being killed by his own crew. Discovering the "new world" was a walk in the park compared to colonizing Mars. Let me dispel a few common misconceptions about Mars itself.

Mars is always moving and can be anywhere from 50 to 250 million miles away. At current flight speeds, it would take a rescue effort between 180 days or up to two years to get there. So, if anything really bad happens to the first crew sent to the red planet, help is a long way away."

"Mars is a planet much like Earth in a lot of ways. But it is much further from the sun and is a cold barren wasteland. The average temperature at the equator is between +50f degrees during the day and -80f degrees at night. At the poles where we think water may be, it is between -80f and -120f degrees below zero."

"If that's not bad enough, Mars has no ozone layer, ionosphere or magnetic field to protect people from deadly solar and cosmic radiation. One solar flare or magnetic storm from the sun, could wipe out all living things on the planet in an instant. Humans cannot survive for very long on a planet without a magnetic field.

If that's not bad enough, Mars has a thin atmosphere that is 90% Co2 and has no standing water. There is evidence that there may have been water on Mars at one time, however, presently there are no oceans, lakes or rivers. In addition, the Martian soil has no nutrients, and any plants grown there, if they survived the harsh conditions, would be poisonous to humans because of cosmic radiation.

If you're seriously thinking about colonizing mars. Think again. You are looking at a world that has no air, no water, no agriculture and is radioactive and poisonous to humans. If that's not bad enough, due to its low gravity and cosmic radiation, it is very unlikely that humans would be able to reproduce on Mars. We would not know until we got there, and risk the birth of horribly deformed offspring

But I have a realistic plan B. A plan to save the human race from the 6th great extinction. Today, I announce to the world, a plan to save the human race and eventually restore earth to its pre-industrial condition. But we will not be going to Mars or trying to colonize the moon. We will colonize space, or more specifically, the space around earth. The Loveton Robotic Corporation has already begun the construction of the first of many Earth orbiting habispheres that will one day soon, be man's last refuge from a dying planet.

More information will follow this announcement and the selection process for those invited to the habisphere colonies will begin. This is Dr. John Loveton from King's Island saying good night and good luck."

As he said this, a large screen video display appeared behind the stage and a CGI video started playing a vision of John's dream. The computer-generated 3D video displayed a world far from earth. A world floating through space with a fantastic wonderland within. A view of a habisphere came into view and through the magic of CGI technology, the image brought the viewer into a vast floating city in the sky. With breathtaking views from low earth orbit 240 miles from the surface. And much like King's Town, there were parks and tree lined streets. Shops and schools, playgrounds and movie theaters. A virtual paradise in space. But only for a few. Only the chosen few would be saved from a dying world.

CHAPTER 26

US president James Brown watched the speech from the ready room in the basement of the White House. He said to no one in particular, "That son of a bitch! Who the hell does he think he is?"

In a hastily assembled meeting were the Secretary of Defense John Mayall, the National Security Adviser Thomas Petty, Secretary of State Paul McCartney and the Director of the CIA Peter Townshend, along with a host of aides. The rest of the cabinet and department heads were on a conference call line listening in.

President got up from his chair and began pacing. A nervous habit no one other than the president enjoyed. "Tom, what's the status at this point?"

Thomas Petty was a professor of law and international studies at Harvard, before the president tapped him to be his national security advisor, a Yale man through and through, he liked wearing bow ties and tweed suits and his horn-rimmed glasses made him look nerdish. "Well sir, we are still accessing the data at this point. We knew about the scheduled launch, and we are just now absorbing the impact of his announcement. Building habispheres in space wasn't really on our radar until now."

Still pacing, the president said, Pete, did your people at the CIA have a clue about this crazy idea? What's a habisphere anyway?"

Pete had the annoying habit of always twirling a pen between his long thick fingers. As he dropped his pen on the floor and picked it up, he said, "My contacts are saying at this point that it's like a small city floating in orbit around the earth, like a space station but much bigger."

The president said, "Get Jim Morrison from NASA on the phone. Maybe he can shed some light on this."

An aid standing behind the president's chair said, "Right away sir."

"John, what does defense have to say?"

"Hell, we are just as surprised as anyone else. We've been watching King's Island for years, but our intel had been slim. There's no imminent military threat. This seems like a 100% civilian project. However, one of our ships was damaged during a reconnaissance mission in the waters off King's Island earlier this year. They have some defensive capabilities but there doesn't appear to be any direct military threat to the US at this point."

Just then an aid said, "We have Morrison on the line, sir."

The president stopped his pacing and said, "Ok patch him through on speaker."

There was a brief pause and then through the tabletop speaker system, the NASA director Jim Morrison said, "Mr. president, Morrison here."

Sitting down at his chair at the head of the table, President Brown said, "Jim, I trust you heard the announcement from King's Island?"

"Yes sir, we are going over the data now. They sent us a standard press release along with some technical data. It's a very ambitious proposal."

Somewhat annoyed the president said, "It's not a proposal Jim, this is real."

"Yes, what I meant sir is whether it's technically possible. Sending thousands of people to live in space is just not something we considered at this point."

"What about the environmental assessment? Is there a real reason for concern?"

Coming through on the conference line the EPA chief Bob Seger said, "The danger of climate change is all too real sir. We've been kicking the can down the road on this one for a long time. It may be time for a carbon policy with some real teeth in it."

The chief political strategist Paula Poundstone through the speaker phone said, "Sir, the poll numbers suggest that only 37% of people who voted in the last election believe in climate change."

Getting really annoyed now the president said, "I don't give a damn about poll numbers. What are the facts? Do we have a crisis here or not?"

"Bob, can EPA get us some real data on this issue?"

"Sir, my department has been politicized by the last three administrations. Most of our genuine researchers left in protest over the last 12 years. The real data is coming from the UN IPCC, the Intergovernmental Panel on Climate Change. They issued a startling report last year. More than 1,000 scientists from around the world signed on. But previous administrations have downplayed the issue to the point that the general public is not concerned."

"Ah um, Mr. President, this is Jim Page from NOAA. The last 10 years have been consecutively the hottest on record and the number and strength of storms has increased exponentially in as many years."

"Mr. President, John Coltrane here from your council of economic advisers. Last year alone, the cost estimate from climate related disasters cost the US alone, 10 billion dollars in damages. That's not including lost wages or productivity."

An exasperated president Brown said, "I've seen the reports but I'm no scientists. Are we really looking at a 6th great extinction? I don't want to be remembered as the president who looked the other way while the whole world fell apart."

Vice President Lakewood on speaker phone said," This has been a long time coming. I remember President Grump famously said, "Climate change is going to be somebody else's problem, not mine."

The President said, "Well it looks like our problem now. Here's what I want. Let's get a team together to look at this from every angle. I want an executive summary of the latest climate data and predictions. We can't just turn off the Co2 spigot, this is going to take years to undo. Paul, I want the State Department to arrange an emergency meeting with all UN members. We have to move on this before it's too late."

One of the president's top aides said from the corner of the room, "What if it's already too late?"

With a worried look, the president glanced at those assembled at the table and said, "Then God help us all!"

All over the world, prime ministers, presidents and cabinet level officials were debating the same issues. John's announcement had set off a frenzy of debate, from the boardroom to the bar room and everywhere in between. The constant babble from the cable news cabal, made John into a hero, saint or villain, depending on which way the wind blew.

Even back on King's Island the debate continued...

CHAPTER 27

After the conference, Kate and Tom retired to Tom's suite while Polly attended the after party. As she walked out on the deck, Kate looking up at the dome of simulated stars said, "Well I think it's time we celebrate, how about some champagne, that was quite a speech don't you think Tom?"

"Yes, mother it was. But don't you think the announcement was a bit premature? What do you think is going to happen now? When word gets out that there are only so many seats on the ark, there's going to be chaos. What's going to happen to the people left behind?"

"Your father can't save everyone dear. This is a last-ditch effort to save the human race from extinction. Maybe this will be a warning, the shot across the bow that the world needs to finally rally together to save the planet."

"The planet will survive mom, it's the people on it that I'm worried about. If dad's predictions are right, who's going to decide who lives and who stays behind to face certain doom? What is he going to do, have a lottery? How's that supposed to work?"

"I don't know but I'm sure your father has thought this through. I would imagine that we have to maintain a diverse gene pool. I would assume they will take a certain number of people from each country. There are roughly 195 countries in the world. If you divide that number by the number of available seats you have your number."

"Mom, you can't just say, ok the 1st 500 people from each country get in line. It will be a catastrophe."

"Yes, you're right dear, a lottery sounds like the best idea. A lottery of the world's best and brightest from as diverse a group as possible. I think *Mother* should decide. She's the most advanced supercomputer in the world. You can't really ask a single person or even a group of people to make that kind of decision. The selection process should be as fair as possible. People should meet a certain set of criteria, then have a lottery or some such thing."

"People are going to complain no matter what you do."

"That's true dear."

"But what if people don't want to go. It's a huge risk.

People don't leave a building before it's on fire, and they don't jump from windows until it's burning down. People may now realize that climate change is real, but how do you convince them that the danger is life threatening and that to save the human race they have to abandon their homes to live in outer space?"

"I don't know. The entire project won't be completed for several years, we may have to wait until things start to get really bad before people decide to leave. Anyway, there's plenty of time to figure these things out. By the way, your father said he wants to talk to you tomorrow."

"What about?"

"I'm not sure dear. He said he wants you to be a part of all this, what he wants you to do I don't know. There are lots of moving parts here. Me, I'm staying out of the whole thing. I've made my contribution. I'm getting too old for these kinds of things."

CHAPTER 28

Tom woke the next morning to a call on his smartphone. It was Crystal. "Good morning Tom, I wanted to let you know your dad has you on his schedule today for 9 am. Things were a little confusing after the conference yesterday and he didn't get a chance to talk to you. Do you mind if I stop by at 8:45? That will give us enough time to take a shuttle to his office."

Tom was about to answer when the line went dead. Apparently, he was listening to a recorded message. He put on a robe and walked out onto the brightly lit patio. He noticed a small breakfast buffet was on the side table. *A waiter bot must have already brought in breakfast while he was still sleeping,* he thought, as he poured himself a cup of coffee and looked out over the well landscaped view. He thought, *it's hard to believe all this is under the dome of an ancient volcano.* After a quick breakfast, he showered, dressed and called Polly. Still not sure what to do he said to no one, "Adam are you there."

Again, as if from nowhere and everywhere, a voice in his head said, "Yes Tom, I am always here. How can I assist you?"

"I'd like to call Polly."

"Of course," said the voice, "all you have to do is say who you want to call into your smartphone and the phone will do the rest."

With some apprehension he held his wrist up and said, "Call Polly."

There was a brief pause and then her voice appeared in his mind, "Tom, hi I'm just getting ready what's up?"

"I'm meeting with my dad at nine, what are your plans?"

"I'm going sightseeing with your mom today. There is so much to see and do here. First, we're going deep sea fishing then snorkeling. They have one of the finest reefs here of anywhere in the world. Then if we are up for it, a sunset sail, do you want to join us?"

"Maybe, I don't know exactly what my plans are for today. I'll meet up with you later."

Just then a bell rang from somewhere, and Crystal's face appeared on the wall monitor in the living room. Tom opened the door and said, "My you're are right on time. Please come in, let me just finish my coffee." He couldn't help but notice the short skirt and high heels she was wearing. He said as he took in the view, "Hey, can we get regular news here?"

Turning towards the wall monitor she said, "Of course, we have all the major networks. You just have to say *Adam turn on*, followed by whatever you want. Give it a try."

Feeling a little awkward at his naivety, he said, "Do I talk at the screen, the smart watch, or just say it out loud."

Crystal laughed and said, "Anytime you want, you can talk to Adam. Looking at the screen he said, "Adam, put on CNN."

The screen turned on and CNN appeared. On the screen behind a talking head, was a satellite view of King's Island.

Tom said as he watched the screen, "We must be all over the news today."

Crystal said, "Yes, your fathers' announcement has stunned the world to say the least. Tom, if we're going to stay on schedule, we have to get going. I have a car holding for us."

As Crystal took Tom's arm, they stepped out into the hallway and out into the busy atrium. They walked through the bustling crowd and out onto the street where an autonomous car was waiting for them. As they sat back in their seats the doors closed and the car slowly pulled away from the curb.

They only traveled about ½ a mile when they pulled up to the LRC tower. The car slowed to a stop and as the doors opened a very tall, well-dressed valet was there to help them out of the car. He said to both of them, father is waiting, right this way please. As they followed the valet into the maze like building two more fell in line behind them. As they entered a waiting elevator, the doors closed, and the elevator quickly lowered several floors and came to a stop in a darkened corridor. The valet walked into the hallway and said please follow me. Crystal, never having been in this part of the building was just as surprised as Tom.

They followed the valet to another waiting elevator and as before, they entered, and the doors shut. This time the elevator went sideways, connecting to a tight-fitting monorail connection. As soon as the box was secure, the monorail sped through a series of connecting tunnels. After several minutes, they came to a stop and the doors to the box opened up. The valet, who had stood silently said, "If you will please follow me."

They were ushered down a hallway and through a vault like door where John was sitting in a dimly lit room behind a large oval table where several of John's senior staff were assembled. Behind him were several video monitors showing news outlets from around the world."

As they entered, the valet backed out of the room and closed the inner door. John stood and said, "Welcome, welcome."

Tom noticed that his father had the annoying habit of repeating a phrase twice.

"Tom, please, please let me skip the preliminaries."

Looking at Crystal he said, thank you for bringing Tom here. I won't be needing you for this meeting, please wait outside."

And with that, she smiled at Tom and left. And looking around the room at this staff he said waving his arm, "You should all know my son Tom by now? I will ask you to return to your offices, I need to talk with Tom privately." And with that, as a group they took their laptops and made their way out the door.

John motioned for Tom to sit at a seat near his and said, "Tom, I want to apologize for not making time to see you until now. I have a very busy as you can imagine."

"Yes, dad I understand. Saving the world is a big job."

"It's not the world I'm trying to save Tom."

"I know that dad, it was just a figure of speech. Why all the secrecy? What is the place some kind of safe room?"

"If we were in the White House, this would be called the war room. We have been monitoring communications from around the world and there are some disturbing trends. As with any sea-change event, there are bound to be consequences. And as I expected, there is a backlash against the habisphere program. There has been from the start. That's one of the reasons I kept it a secret for as long as I could."

"We made the first prototype launch last week and it was a resounding success. But the only people who knew about it at the time were government agencies. Now that the general public knows about the program, there are bound to be some skeptics. And yes, even worse, some protesters. A dangerous group called "Earth First," is against the habisphere program and vows to prevent what they call, a robotic takeover of the human race. They claim that my program to save humanity, is a cleverly disguised ploy to enslave the human race and force them to work in mining camps on the Moon or even Mars. Pretty farfetched huh?"

"Well dad, I must say, it's not a far cry from building habispheres in space to save the human race from extinction."

"Yeah, I guess you have a point there. But if it came to it, I have robots better suited for mining the Moon or even Mars. But more importantly there are governments that see us as a threat. They think that I have somehow upset the balance of power that has existed for over 1000 years. Well it was their failure to act that brought us to this point. Anyway, there are others that I'm more concerned about. There are some politically powerful people who say that this is a sign of the second coming and that I'm the anti-Christ."

"Not everyone sees things the way you do dad."

"I know. And that has always been my problem. Anyway, I didn't ask you here to talk about me. I want to talk about you. I know you have been through quite an ordeal in the last few days. I'm sure you have a ton of questions for me, but I must ask that you wait for things to settle down first."

"Well Dad, I do have a few questions that need to be addressed now."

"Ok, what are they? I've got a lot on my plate right now."

"To start with, how long do we have, I mean before it's too late. Too late to do anything about climate change?"

"It's already too late son. Why do you think I set all this in motion? This is all carefully planned to coincide with the end of humanity. By the time phase one is complete, people will be begging to get off the earth. Take a look at this image."

He turned in his seat and said, "Adam, show us the latest polar satellite images please."

There was a brief pause and the main screen behind John displayed the images from the northern pole from the last 50 years. The video showed a gradual shift through time as the polar ice sheet receded, returned then receded again. The cycle was repeated several times until the polar cap and sea ice vanished completely.

"What we have here Tom, is the loss of what is known as the albedo effect, essentially the beginning of the end. The albedo effect is the amount of sunlight that is reflected off the polar sea ice. At its height, about 150 years ago, the albedo effect accounted for a reflection nearly 60% of the sunlight reaching earth from both poles. Without that reflection, all that solar energy will be absorbed into the oceans, increasing global temperatures by as much as 3 to 5 degrees in just a few years. And that is a conservative estimate. And that's all it will take. Game over. After that, things will get out of hand fairly quickly."

"Yes dad, I've read the data. Warmer oceans mean more frequent and stronger storms. What's the big deal."

"Yes, higher ocean temps mean more frequent and more powerful storms, but there is another even more devastating effect. Warming oceans will cause a destruction of the coral reefs around the world. Even a slight increase in ocean temperature can have a devastating effect on a reef. All it takes is a change of 1.8 degrees f to cause a massive die-off. Once this happens, it's only a matter of time before the whole self-sustaining system goes out of whack. From the very small micro-organisms that live in the coral reefs to small reef fish and larger predators. It's all interconnected. And without coral reefs to keep kelp beds in check, they will overpopulate the coasts, causing ocean dead zones where oxygen depletion will cause massive species die-offs.

After that, it's the end of life on earth as we know it. Without a healthy ocean, the larger mammals like us can't survive. When atmospheric oxygen levels drop below 18%, that's it for humans. Small land animals and reptiles will survive, but we won't. My best estimate is that we have between 3 to 5 years before the ocean's oxygen regeneration system completely collapses. It may happen sooner than that. It's a very complicated system. Emerging economies are causing an unpredictable increase in gas trapping Co2 emissions every year."

Tom shifted nervously in his seat and said, "What can I do to help?"

John turned back around in his desk chair and looking Tom in the eye said, "Tom I know you're coming to the party a little late. But I have a very important job for you, you and Polly both if you want. I would like you to be my ambassadors so to speak, for the integration program. As my VP of Passenger Integration, you will be my eyes and ears on the new habisphere when it's completed. Until then, I want you to be in charge of the selection process. This is a most critical position that will require a set of diplomatic skills that I obviously lack. I truly believe that you are up to the task. What do you think? You and Polly make a great team. Where did you find her anyway?"

"We were neighbors on Nantucket, remember the Johnsons?"

"Oh, that's right, she was the cute little redhead you had a crush on if I remember."

"Yes dad, that was a long time ago."

"But still, she's proven herself to be very resourceful."

"Yes, she saved my ass more than once. As I said before, I'll help you in any way I can. I'm just worried about the repercussions. There will be so many people left behind."

"Yes, that's true, but think about it this way. There will be a great number of people that won't want to leave; won't want to leave family or loved ones behind. Another group, you know the type. Just won't leave. These are the ones who refuse to evacuate when a dangerous storm is approaching and stay behind, only to die or be rescued later at great expense. Then there are the old and infirm, and those not healthy enough to make the trip. There are another group of those who don't believe in global warming and like a frog in a pot of slowly boiling water. They won't jump out and will die. Then there are the deeply religious. They believe the ancient texts and see this as a sign of the second coming and that The Christ is returning to bring them into heaven. Others just aren't genetically fit. We can't have sociopaths or schizophrenics trying to adapt to a new life in space, it would be too dangerous. So, when you start to narrow it down, there is really only a handful of people that will actually qualify and want to go."

"But dad, were talking about a population of almost 8 billion people. How many will you be able to save?"

"Tom, it's not a question of how much we can save, but the genetic diversity and the quality of the people we will save. It will take a long time for the earth to rebound. Once it does, we will need a strong, intelligent and resilient population to repopulate the earth. We're talking hundreds, maybe thousands of years. That's a long time to wait, a lot will happen. It's a huge risk. We, and I mean "we" as a species, might not survive this. Adapting to life in space will not be easy.

"Ok, when do I start?"

"We are still about a year away from the first habispheres completion. What I want you to focus on, is the selection process and family integration. Our research suggests that people will be better able to cope with the adjustment to living in space, as a family unit. Think of it as a built-in support group. The best grouping is going to look like a typical family unit. Husband and wife, or mother, father and kids. Maybe a grandparent if they are fit enough. We aren't planning to be a nursing home in space, however, in some of the more advanced cultures, grandparents are seen as an important part of the family cohesiveness."

"We have *Mother* working on an algorithm to assist in the selection process. But we have to balance the obvious benefit to using computer programming to solve this problem, without the appearance that computers are running everything. Most people are not ready for the future of AI, even though it is already here."

"What do you mean already here?"

"Tom didn't you know? This place is completely automated by the most advanced AI quantum computer in the world. Did you know that *Mother* is in complete control of this entire complex? From the HVAC, lighting, traffic and power, to food production, processing and distribution; they are all controlled by advanced AI. She controls everything, including our production facilities both here and at our drone factory in New Zealand. She also controls all the robots, humanoids and automated systems. She even controls our satellite launch program. There isn't a single thing here that doesn't have her fingerprint on it. A lot of people outside this place would be concerned by that. So, we have to at least appear to be in control."

"What do you mean, appear to be in control?"

"Do you remember the pictures from NASA, when they landed the first men on the moon. There were dozens of people at consoles and stations, all appeared to be deeply involved in some part of the mission. Most of them were just there for show. Once the capsule was put into orbit, where wasn't much anyone could do other than watch. It's much the same here. We have a NASA looking control room, with fancy looking equipment and people staring at monitors. But *Mother* is doing all the heavy lifting. The important looking people, the equipment, it's all for show."

"But what if something goes wrong? Aren't you worried about, I don't know, some kind of robotic uprising? Adam said that there is an advanced robotic society here. What if they get tired of being our slaves?"

"Tom, let me set aside some of your fears. I created this robotic society for the benefit of mankind. The three laws of robotics are built into the hardware of every computerized and robotic system here."

"But don't you have robots making robots? What if there's a glitch, a malfunction or a conflict in programing? Aren't you taking a big risk, putting everything in the hands of an autonomous machine? Shouldn't the ultimate decisions be made by people; I mean real people? I'm not saying this is going to happen, but what if there was a war. What if you had to defend yourself from some kind of attack. Would you leave life and death decisions up to a machine?"

"Tom, we have already been attacked. My defensive forces run by *Mother* are second to none. When the world sees what we've done here, there will be no more wars. No one should needlessly lose their life due to a breakdown in diplomacy. AI is man's final salvation."

"Dad, I'm not talking about a breakdown in diplomacy. Before I came here, I was briefed at the highest level of the US government. There are some in positions of power, that want to nuke this place. They think King's Island and the technology you have created here, pose a threat to world peace."

"I know. Listen Tom, there are always going to be powerful forces that are resistant to change. When the US government made the decision to enter WWII. President Roosevelt sat down with the CEOs of every car company in America. They knew about the decision to go to war and were ready to cooperate in any way they could. Roosevelt thanked them and said, *that is not enough.*"

"They looked around the room at each other and the president said, "I'm going to make it illegal to make cars in America until after the war." They balked, and then sued. But his executive order was upheld by the Supreme Court. That forced the car makers to switch all their production capacity to the war effort. They all became DeFacto defense contractors. Roosevelt knew that the only way to defeat the German army was an all-out effort. That was real leadership. We don't have that today. Even now, with an all-out effort, there is nothing we can do to stop severe climate change. They have the same research available that I do. They just either can't admit it to themselves or are too entrenched in their own beliefs to see the forest for the trees."

"Believe me, when oxygen levels start dropping, they will come around, we are mankind's last option. Why do you think I built this facility so far from civilization? We are protected by 3000 miles of open ocean in every direction."

"Yes, you could say that is true for America too, and look what happened on 911."

"Tom, events like 911 are exactly why we need advance AI. To be able to look at all the available data objectively, and not cherry-pick what fits into a preconceived idea of reality. The data was there. But due to the compartmentalization of data in the US government, it prevented any one person from seeing the whole picture. 911 could have been prevented. Why do you think no one asked about a group of young, middle eastern, Muslim men, wanted to learn to fly a jet liner, but not land?"

"Ok I get it dad. Humans don't always match up to the challenges we face, we make mistakes. But that is what makes us human."

"Son, listen. This is our future. One day soon, AI will take over the destiny of the human race. Think about where we are today? Humans are destroying the very planet on which they need to survive. It was not a conscious or willful decision. Mr. and Mrs. John Doe didn't just wake up one day and say, "*Today I'm going to destroy the planet everyone follow me.*" It happened over a long period of general complacency. Right now, as a society, we struggle to make the big decisions for ourselves. We will need an AI overseer to get us past this point in our evolution or we will not survive. Right now, AI is our only hope."

"I wish you were wrong dad; I really do."

"Have you thought about population control?"

"No, not recently why?"

"The overpopulation of the human race is the real cause of climate change. Our inability to control birth rates put a strain on the earth's natural resources. The history books are filled with accounts of humans decimating natural resources until the resources are depleted and the community dies. The Incas are a perfect example. They had a robust and successful civilization, and their prosperity led to a huge increase in the population. That is always the beginning of the end. To meet the needs of a growing citizenry, they clear cut all the forests to build homes for their growing population. When the seasonal rains came, it washed away all the soil and their crops failed. Their entire population died from starvation."

"We will face the same fate in the habispheres if we don't limit the population. People of childbearing age will have to be on mandatory contraception. *Mother* will decide if and when a couple may conceive. As on earth, there are only so many seats on the Ark. In addition, pregnancies in less than 1g have to be controlled very carefully. It will take generations for humans to adapt to childbirth in space."

"I see that there are aspects to this that I need to get up to speed on."

"Yes, don't worry, you have plenty of time. I have downloaded files to your cloud account to get you up to speed. You can log in to any device using your iris scan. That's all for now, I'm already late for a video conference meeting with the Pope. We'll talk later. If you ever have any questions, just ask Adam. He is actually a human interactive interface for *Mother*. And you can always reach me via your smart watch."

At that moment Crystal appeared and led Tom back to the monorail. "I trust you had a good meeting?" she said as they boarded the monorail.

"Yes, it was very enlightening," Tom said as he reached for a handrail to steady himself as the sleek craft slowly made its way through the labyrinth of tunnels under King's Island.

Tom returned to his suite and put on the news. The 24-news cycle was buzzing with the implications of John's announcement. The talking heads from around the world were in rare form, debating this and that. Who should go, who shouldn't. Was it going too far? Would anyone abandon earth before any real danger existed. Was it madness or foresight? Was he a genius ahead of his time or a deranged lunatic? There was admiration and criticism from all sides.

Tom thought back to his students and their families and how all this was going to impact the average person on the street.

CHAPTER 29

The world was in an uproar following John's speech and the first announced launch. World leaders demanded a more detailed explanation of what exactly the intent of the LRC habisphere program was, and what the selection process would be. True to his word, John, through the LRC PR office, issued White Paper statements about his plans to save humanity. John Loveton's genius was recognized the world over and he was the first ever multiple Nobel prize winner. As the habispheres were under construction, world leaders were begging for access to the selection process for those who would live in the new space colonies. Due to the limited number of seats available, the LRC planned a lottery for the first habisphere. In a press release and subsequent press briefings, the LRC stated that only the best and brightest of mankind would be selected from as diverse a group as possible.

As rocket after rocket was launched from King's Island, and hundreds of spaced based industrial 3D printers worked day and night and construction of the first habisphere was completed ahead of schedule. LRC released a video showing the incredible views of the habisphere as the first human inhabitants were scheduled for processing.

The United Nations held an emergency meeting regarding the habispheres and diplomats from every nation implored the LRC for more open access to reservations. John held a video conference with world leaders at the UN and made it very clear that those government and industry leaders who continued to fight against climate change legislation, would not be invited to join the new habisphere community.

Following his announcement, world leaders from every nation protested the selection process. Threats were made against the LRC and Three Kings Island. Through the world court, Three Kings Island declared separate nation status and petitioned the UN for recognition and protection as a UN member. The LRC also declared the future habispheres as a sovereign nation of orbiting states of the DEEP (democracy for earth's environmental protection).

US war ships already in the south pacific threatened to shoot down any rockets launched from Kings Island, unless the US government had a say in who was allowed to go. The LRC announced that they would continue with the scheduled launches and stated that any nations that interfered with future launches would be dealt with accordingly. Unbeknownst to world leaders, the LRC had implemented a space-based laser security system, protecting the launch pad, rockets, Islands and habispheres from attack.

The US tried to shoot down an LRC rocket from a destroyer off the coast of Australia. The missile was destroyed, and the destroyer was damaged by an armed LRC satellite using an advanced laser guided gamma ray weapon. The LRC announced that any future attacks will be seen as an act of war against the DEEP (democracy for earth's environmental protection).

New Zealand admonished the US attack as an unprovoked aggression on a sovereign nation and appealed to the UN for sanctions against the US and warned that any nation that attempted to interfere with future launches will be banned from the habispheres entirely.

In retaliation for the damage to the destroyer, the US launched a covert commando attack on Three King's Island. All the soldiers were captured by the LRC robotic army and were safely returned via an advanced autonomous stealth drone capable of supersonic speed. Flaunting US law in restricted air space, the commandos were returned directly to the White House helipad. The radar evading drone took off and easily out maneuvered the top US air force fighter jets and returned unscathed to Three Kings Island. The embarrassed President was forced to apologize on national TV and the world was introduced to the full technical power of the LRC now known as the United Republic of King's Island.

Following the first habisphere lottery, riots occurred around the world when people realized that only a small fraction of the earth's population would be invited to the limited space available in the habisphere colonies. The world's wealthiest families attempted to buy their way into the habispheres but were denied access. Through a team of press spokesmen, the LRC, again and again, explained the qualifications for applications to join the habisphere community. The LRC would accept only the best and brightest from an equal cross-section of humanity. With the emphasis on maintaining as diverse a population as possible. A team of specialists was sent to every country around the world searching for the "chosen few" who will help create the first generation of non-terrestrial humans.

CHAPTER 30

Following the completion of the first habisphere, the very first flights brought up teams of humanoids hosts to prepare the Hab for the first colonists. Advanced passenger planes capable of ground to space flight, were being dispatched from New Zealand to nations all around the world to transport the "chosen few" to Hab 1.

Tom and Polly were on the first passenger flight to the floating city in the sky. Tom, as VP in charge of the New Habisphere Integration Program, was the face of the LRC. Although he had reservations about leaving earth, he knew what was a stake and he did his best to integrate the 300 new arrivals to Hab 1.

The entire Los Angeles airport was under heavy security prior to departure. The threats received by the LRC numbered in the thousands. Most were crackpots, and easily dismissed, others were more serious. The "Earth First" movement had gained traction and had already carried out huge demonstrations across the world demanding an end to what they called, the first step of human enslavement by AI machines. Religious cults cropped up using scripture to gain followers and proselytize about the end of the world. The real danger was from fundamentalist radicals, who saw the habispheres as a violation of their faith and a blasphemy against god.

Taking no chances on their maiden voyage, Tom had their own security forces scanning the iris biometric ID of everyone in and out of the LA airport for weeks prior to the scheduled departure. Prior to take-off LRC agents were scattered throughout the airport.

Tom and Polly were seated in the forward cabin on the first of its kind jumbo space jet. Using both turbo fan engines, and chemical booster rockets, the craft lifted off like a plane, and as it reached the stratosphere, chemical booster rockets kicked in and propelled the craft out of the earth's gravity and into outer space.

Nervous and excited, first group of Hab 1 colonists waited patiently as the stewards gave the last-minute pre-flight instructions. The all clear was given by the tower and with US air force fighter jets as an escort, the huge LRC space jet rumbled off the runway. The plane gained altitude quickly and maneuvered to an altitude of 50,000 ft where there was a brief pause, when the booster rockets pushed the plane out of the stratosphere and into the exosphere, where craft floated free from earth's gravity and reached a speed of 28 thousand miles per hour. The views were incredible as the now space-based plane turned over 180 degrees towards earth and prepared to dock with the rotating habisphere.

The habisphere, a beautiful floating city in the sky, orbited 18 thousand feet above the earth, was in constant rotation to create a simulated gravity. The 600 hundred passengers were escorted on board and shown to their quarters without incident. A few passengers were space sick due to the weightless environment, but the team was prepared for that and specialized vacuums were on hand to suck up any floating debris.

Tom and Polly acted like ambassadors and greeted as many newcomers as possible. Hab 1 had a Central Park with a lake surrounded by grass and tree lined paths. And as part of a celebration, a concert in the park with a fireworks display was planned for later that night.

"This was an incredible day. I'm exhausted," Polly said as they made their way to their new apartment. Their luggage had already been delivered to their room and unpacked by their personal valet. Tom was tired from glad-handing the hundreds of colonists who arrived with them. He stepped out on the balcony, poured himself a glass of water from a crystal pitcher on a side table and looked out over the interior of the hab. He saw a city in the sky, floating far above a world in chaos.

The months leading up to the first flight, saw a population in turmoil. The world watched 24-hour news as the selection process for the first colonists was completed. And as the realization set in, that so many were going to be left behind, the real protests started. Angry that the world's leaders failed to respond to a growing threat in time to do anything about it. And now that the imminent danger of climate change became all too real, people were protesting in the streets in large numbers. In smaller unstable countries, governments were overthrown. Coups and attacks against once powerful leaders upended democracies and dictatorships across the globe.

Civil war broke out across the middle east, and martial law was declared in countries on almost every continent.

CHAPTER 31

Meanwhile on Hab 1 the reports from social media of every kind, gave rave reviews for the advancement in technology created by LRC.

----

*"I love my new apartment. Every detail
is thoughtfully considered."*

"The food is excellent up here and free!"

*"I couldn't be happier; I struggled every day to feed my
kids and keep them safe. But here in the space colonies,
they have the best schools, free health care,
and I'm having my hip replaced."*

"I love playing zero gravity sky ball, it's the coolest!"

The accolades on hab-news and social media went on and on, only spurring more discontent from the billions of people not selected.

Meanwhile, things on earth were turning for the worse. The citizens chosen for the habispheres could do nothing but watch as the earth rapidly descended into the chaos.

All over the world, John's dire predictions were starting to come true. Across the globe, severe storms, fueled by ocean temperature increases battled coastal regions. Those storms in turn, fueled inland storms and spawned thousands of tornados and destroyed urban areas and productive farmland across the globe. Sea level rise reached

15 feet in some areas, flooding coastal cities around the world. Crops were failing, and farm animals were dying in unprecedented numbers from extreme heat and drought.

Due to a rapid increase in ocean acidification, once plentiful ocean fisheries started a massive die off and even small island nations couldn't feed their people. Intense drought followed by heat lightning caused wildfires around the world, and serious famine ravaged Africa and Southeast Asia.

In America, the President by executive order, declared Martial Law and stopped all foreign food contracts and began to stockpile and ration food stocks for a nation of nearly 600 million people. Governments all over the world struggled to maintain order as chaos spread to nearly every corner of the globe.

Private yachts sailed the dangerous waters off the coast of New Zealand attempting to dock at Three Kings port. Several were damaged by the LRC naval defense force, and the rest left for their home ports.

A host of countries, angered with the habisphere selection process, attempted a naval blockade of the island and the LRC was forced to retaliate by sinking several ships with secrete marine drones.

The US through the UN sued the LRC in the World Court for violating the ban on weapons in space and through intermediaries, the LRC disclosed classified documents from Russia, China and the US, that they already had less effective but still dangerous space-based weapons of their own. The lawsuit was promptly dropped.

Private space companies attempted to compete with LRC launches. Rockets were built, and were tickets sold, with the promise of admission to the habisphere colony. The LRC tried to discredit the would-be space entrepreneurs with warnings and public awareness ads on all forms of social media. The plans went ahead anyway and when the first private space capsule tried to dock with a habisphere still under construction. The ship was turned away by LRC's robotic security forces, and all on board were killed when they attempted earth re-entry. Following the accident, no further attempts were made for unauthorized flights to the habispheres.

CHAPTER 32

After several years, 20 habispheres containing 50,000 souls in each were completed and all of the 1,000,000 occupants were in place.

Due to a complete collapse of the world's healthcare infrastructure, infectious diseases ravaged the remaining population adding to the chaos and misery. All over the world, millions of people either died from disease, starvation or from wars and urban warfare. What was left of the human race on earth, devolved to a point of tribal warfare and a struggle for survival. The remaining humans lived like their ancestors had during the last ice age 15,000 years ago. Warring tribes struggling for survival in a world of dwindling resources.

Gaia herself was in her final death throes. Due to a worldwide drought, wildfires destroyed 40% of the world's forests, releasing even more stored carbon and reducing one of the largest oxygen producing engines in the world to less than ½ of its pre-industrial level.

The increased levels of Co2 in the atmosphere caused a corresponding increase in temperatures and ocean acidification, which killed off the last of earth's coral reefs. This completed the downward spiral of overall ocean health. With the last of the coral reefs gone, the biodiversity that had sustained a healthy ecosystem for over a billion years completely collapsed. Without coral reefs to keep kelp beds in check, oxygen depleted ocean dead zones caused a massive die off of nearly all shallow water reef fisheries. The combined destruction of the ocean's biodiversity set in motion the total collapse of the ocean's oxygen regeneration system.

The earth receives 70% of its oxygen from the worlds' oceans. Without healthy oceans, the earth's atmospheric oxygen levels plunged rapidly killing off most of the larger mammals including what was left of the human race.

In the same way a family abandons a sick animal at the vets. People in the habispheres, had already said goodbye to their loved ones, and made peace with the fact that the fate of those left behind, was out of their hands. When the last of the remaining humans died, they went on with their new lives in the habisphere colonies as if nothing happened.

CHAPTER 33

In the new space colonies, every task, job or function was performed by robots or automated by machines. Humans were now free from the arduous never-ending work of their predecessors.

For centuries humans toiled for food, shelter and clothing, and in the last century, worked 40 to 50 hours a week, mostly living paycheck-to-paycheck to provide for themselves and their families.

Yet back on earth, they had challenges and obstacles to overcome. They had a sense of purpose, they felt satisfaction from a job well done, had a sense of belonging. Without these challenges, humans began a slow evolutionary change adapting to life in space.

The first generation of non-terrestrial humans struggled to adapt to the new realities of living in space with robotic servants performing every task.

The more creative and intelligent, made use of their newfound free time by exploring their passion for the arts, music, or whatever their interests were.

However, those who had difficulty adapting, resorted to heavy drinking or synthetic drug use. For others, living in a floating island in space circling the earth was too much for their terrestrial minds and bodies cope with. They either committed suicide or went insane and were sent back to earth.

In the habisphere colonies, robots or machine automation, took the place of human labor. Humans were now free to do whatever they pleased. For first generation of terrestrial humans, those that were able to adapt, life was like a paradise in space.

The habispheres, were constructed with as many Earth-like amenities as possible. Each habisphere had parks with grass and trees, ponds and playgrounds for kids, pedestrian walkways, restaurants, shops and movie theaters. Everything a modern city had on earth was provided for in the new habisphere colonies, and everything a human could wish for was provided by their robotic hosts.

However, the freedom to live life without the constant need to provide, was like a double-edged sword. For thousands of years, humans had a function. A place in society, a job, or a role to play as a doctor, teacher, baker or attorney or any of the many functions that were no longer needed in the space colonies.

So, groups of colonists formed labor committees, to allow those who chose to work in their profession, could do so. They could work side by side with like-minded humans, or a mix of humans and humanoids. Bakers could run a bakery, or chefs could open a restaurant. For some, humans couldn't be replaced by robots and there was a separate system setup for those that preferred a human touch. These fields were mostly in the areas of medicine.

Even the task of parenting was eventually taken over by robotic caregivers; who would never become tired, or angry or scold their child, or drink too much and become violent. Even childbirth was delegated to the robotically controlled birthing labs. Where births were planned according to the needs of the colony. Even traits and characteristics of each child could be selected by parents like items on a menu of preferred attributes.

Brown hair, check. Green eyes, check. Carmel skin, check. High intelligence, check. Nonviolent tendencies, check. Prior to conception, all the undesirable traits of human evolution were just programed out of the human genome genetically. Over time, psychological disabilities like autism and schizophrenia were simply engineered out of the human species.

In addition, through genetic engineering and CRISPR technology, inherited diseases became a thing of the past. A tweak here and a tweak there, on a pair of DNA strands, and you had the perfect human being.

CHAPTER 34

After the accident at the lab in the early days of the habisphere project, John Loveton was severely injured and on life support. His lungs, liver, pancreas and kidneys were badly damaged, and he lost both legs, an arm and one eye. Through experiments in biomedical engineering, the genetics lab was able to grow the organs he needed using his own DNA. By growing organs from his own cells, they were able to manufacture new organs and saved his life. After his recovery from several organ transplant surgeries, he was fitted with advanced robotic prosthetics to replace his lost limbs and eye.

Following Dr. Loveton's injury, he realized that with continued advancements in AI and robotics, robots would one day outlive humans' beings and become the sole intelligent life in the universe.

He saw the unlimited potential that a robotic humanoid could have. Not only were the advanced humanoids better at everything. They were smarter, faster and stronger. They would never age or get sick. He realized that technology would reach a singularity. Or a point at which either through advances in cellular genetics or advanced robotics, humans could live forever. Immortality was in his grasp.

In order to avoid the inevitable robotic takeover of the human race, he began experiments transplanting cloned human brains into humanoid bodies to make the transition from organic humans to humanoid robots with naturally born human brains.

Starting on mice, he began a brain transplant program using newly designed nerve synopsis regeneration. By getting the cells of the central nervous system to regenerate at the molecular level, a brain could be transplanted the same way a heart or kidney was. After several successful transplants in mice, and against the strict rules governing experiments on human cloning. Dr. Loveton with his assistant Dr Ohm, begin secret experiments transplanting cloned human brains into robotic bodies. Working in secret and using robotic surgeons their attempts at first failed miserably. The experiments yielded Frankenstein like monsters which were promptly destroyed.

They continue the secret project using advanced quantum computers and robotic surgeons. After several trials, they eventually perfected the process of linking the synapses of the brain with an organic gel developed from cephalopods. Dr. Loveton had his brain successfully transferred into a humanoid body. Violating colonial law against human cloning, he became the first successful human brain transplant, making him virtually immortal.

Following Dr. Loveton's successful brain transplant, he returned to his personal habisphere where he hacked Dr. Ohm's research files. Hidden in the files he discovered plans to create a secret army of cloned humanoids. Continuing the banned practice of human cloning, Dr. Ohm planned to insert cloned human brains into specialized humanoid bodies. Fearing the backlash of project, he knew was imminent.

The project was discovered by authorities and his secret lab was raided. All the lab equipment was seized, and Dr Ohm was banished to a mining station on the Moon. The new Dr. Loveton denied any knowledge of the project and went on as if nothing had happened.

CHAPTER 35

Over time, each of the 20 habispheres were modified for a specific purpose to provide goods and services for the habisphere community.

There were habispheres designed for agriculture, recycling, waste treatment and water recycling. Others were designed for recreation, one for science and bioengineering, one for computer programing, another for medical and life sciences.

Similar to their sister cities, each habisphere or hab, as they were called, evolved a separate culture and value system, according to its role and function in the colony.

In the early days, the colony operated without a centralized government. There was a honeymoon period which lasted a couple of years, when everything was shiny and new, and people were still adapting to life in space. Until internal squabbling and divisions among various factions within the colonies led to the same type of feuding and infighting which doomed earth to an eternally slow death.

As time went on, it became obvious that some kind of a centralized government was needed to iron out disputes within and between habs. A colonial government was formed based loosely on both the US Constitution and the British Parliamentary system. Each Hab had elections for local (within the Hab) and state (outside each hab) for representation on the new colonial government.

Along with the unintended "class system" came with it the political strife and turmoil that dominated earth's culture wars of which epitomized human interaction since the dawn of civilization.

Without purposely creating a class system, one evolved from the division of labor among the separate "habs" as they became known. Even though robots and machines had taken over nearly every aspect of habisphere functions, humans still felt the need to have control over the management of the systems in each Hab. So, to pacify the need for humans to feel like they were in charge, committees were formed in each habisphere to influence the decision-making process in any otherwise automated self-governing system. And people were appointed or chosen to oversee basically autonomous habisphere functions to make them feel important.

Then over time, tensions between the habispheres arose. The recycling hab felt that they didn't have enough parks to walk in. The repair and maintenance hab felt that they should have better accommodations. The medical hab thought that they should be paid more by the way of perks, than the other habs, and so on.

CHAPTER 36

As time went on, and a new generation of non-terrestrial humans were born into the colony. The new generation, and the generations to follow, became more and more adapted to life in space. As the humans adapted to life in space, they begin a separate evolutionary tree.

They became smaller in stature, smaller boned, and required less calories. The cranial structure of the human head changed to accommodate a more weightless environment. With less gravity, blood flowed more to the brain, therefore the human head expanded in size accordingly. And without the constant challenges that the old earth required. Humans relied more and more on their humanoid hosts and therefore humans became less intelligent and more passive.

The change in human anatomy changed so slowly over time, the slight changes from generation to generation were barely noticed.

With the eventual de-evolution of human beings, robots advanced to the point that they were given the power and authority to watch over and protect humans at any cost. The three laws of robotics were integrated into the hardware of every robot in the solar system.

1. A robot may not injure a human being or, through inaction, allow a human being to come to harm.

2. A robot must obey orders given it by human beings except where such orders would conflict with the First Law.

3. A robot must protect its own existence as long as such protection does not conflict with the First or Second Law.

CHAPTER 37

On the desolate Moon mining station, Dr Ohm had to start his research all over again. Despite repeated failures, he continued the experiments until he was able to perfect the process again. He had a specialized humanoid body made and he successfully transferred his own brain into a robotic body.

As his research in advanced robotics progressed, Dr Ohm created a robotic army with the sole purpose of protecting himself from the threat from the habisphere colonies. He modified the humanoid bodies with technological advances like Wi-Fi, scanners, wireless communication, hard drives, weightless, and gravity propulsion, lasers and other weapons. These humanoid robots he called Humbots. They were designed as warriors and were controlled exclusively by Dr. Ohm and his generals.

The new Humiods however, were found to have the unanticipated negative aspects of human evolution. The ability to think and reason brought with it the innate characteristics of humans. Gandhi and Dr. King, along with Hitler, Stalin, and Manson. The good and the evil.

Fearing a vote by the colonial government that would control the destiny of his new cloned brain humanoid colony, Dr Ohm's rogue army of militarized robots planned to attack the habispheres.

Dr Ohm lost control of the Humoids under his command and they end up turning on him. As he tried to warn the habispheres of the danger, he was attacked by his own creation and left to die. As he lay dying, he sent out a flash message to Dr Loveton in his personal habisphere that his army went rouge and were in route to earth.

The habisphere colonies had existed peacefully for years and there was never a need for an army or military of any kind. When the Humbot army attacked, the habisphere colonies were completely defenseless. The humanoid robots in the colonies did their best to defend the humans, but they were no match for Dr Ohm's militarized Humbots. Once the Humbots had defeated the colony humanoids, the humans were slaughtered by the thousands.

The fear of being hunted by Dr. Ohm's rouge army, left the survivors two choices, both bad. Stay and face certain death by the hands of a rogue army of killer robots or take their chances on a voyage 4.3 light years in space and save what's left of the human race from extinction. The few survivors banded together and took control of the colonies interstellar ships designed to search the nearest star system for habitable planets and left the solar system forever.

Dr Loveton could only watch in horror as Dr Ohm's militarized robotic army attacked the habisphere colonies. In a matter of a few hours most of the habispheres were destroyed and the remaining humans left for Alpha Centauri. Loveton's horror turned to shock when he realized his invention for the salvation of man was eventually used as a weapon to destroy it.

After the exodus, Dr Loveton revealed that he was living in a humanoid body and the colony humanoids he created took him in like family. With his help, the remaining robots in the habisphere community hunted down Dr Ohm. He was found half dead, on a Moon mining station and although he transferred his brain into a humanoid body, he still required oxygen and basic nutrients to survive. He had been injured beyond help and revealed that the Humoids, had taken over his robotic army of Humbots and turned on him. As he lay dying, with his last breath he gave over the encrypted codes that controlled the Humbot central computer control system.

With that data in hand, the colony humanoids were able to reprogram Dr Ohm's robotic army to hunt and destroy the last of the Humoids and bring peace back to the solar system.

After the Habisphere War and Exodus, under the direction of Dr. Loveton, the remaining robots pooled their resources and rebuilt what was left of the habispheres. Out of the 20 built by the Loveton Robotic Corp, they were able to piece together 5 habispheres from the wreckage.

Naturally born humans became extinct and the solar system was populated by robots for 400 years. During that time, the robots created an advanced culture. With their original programming still intact, they focused on restoring the earth, and complete Dr Loveton's dream, that one day, if any remaining humans could be found, they could be restored to their rightful place in the universe and repopulate the earth in a garden of Eden.

But there were some within the robotic hierarchy, that thought of humans like a virus. And that if they were allowed back on earth, over time they would inevitably repeat the same mistakes, and destroy the earth all over again.

The End of Book I

BOOK II

CHAPTER 1

The survey and mining ship Forward and its crew of 20, were on a 10-year deep space survey mission to locate and extract "rare earth" mineral deposits on the moons of Jupiter.

Due to the length of the 7-year voyage, the crew was placed in extended hibernation. While in flight, the ship was controlled by a small team of AI robots.

In a celestial dance of the heavens. Every 400 years, the planets in our solar system align causing the release of a graviton, a single powerful gravitational wave.

As the ship passed between Europa and Jupiter, the powerful wave hit the ship knocking out the command and control systems and the ship was cast adrift, only to be caught in the gravitational pull of Jupiter's moons, Europa and Ganymede and held there for 400 years.

The plutonium power system providing life support to the captain and crew remained functioning, while the ships command and control systems went offline indefinitely. Another 400 years pass, and the planets realign, and the process is repeated. The ship was hit by another graviton and this time the ship's command and control systems were reactivated. The ship, once caught between the gravity of two moons, is pushed out into space floating freely.

CHAPTER 2

From the bridge of a robotically controlled salvage ship, a rare earth mining vessel from earth's distant past was discovered floating adrift in Jupiter's orbit.

Due to the danger of wireless virus infiltration. All communication and ships operations are done manually by autonomous humanoid robots.

The fight supervisor, a humanoid robot radioed the advanced humanoid captain, *"Inform the Captain, an intact ship from the Habisphere era has been found. We will attempt to capture the ship and bring it onboard."*

The salvage ship, searching the gas giants for debris from the habisphere wars, which scattered thousands of pieces of space junk careening throughout the solar system, was controlled by a team of robots, each designed with a specific purpose based on the design of the Union of Robotic Design and Manufacturing Committee.

The ship's robotic captain, an advanced humanoid, was part of the upper class of robots, delegated with the control functions of the salvage ship. Advances in robotic technology had reached a point where the advanced humanoid control robots were indistinguishable from their original human creators' warts and all.

The bridge control bot reported, *"Captain, markings indicate the ships call-sign is indeed from the habisphere era. We are bringing the ship on board."*

The newly discovered ship was scanned, analyzed and brought aboard the huge salvage ship through the use of robot tender ships. The humanoids boarded the ship and found a crew of 20 humans in extended hibernation. The humans were examined, and a report was created for study before a decision is made by The Robotic Council High Command, regarding what to do.

The robotically controlled salvage ship was not prepared to house and feed 20 naturally born humans, so a decision was made by the High Council of Inner Solar System Control, that the humans would be kept in hibernation until a committee decision was made on what to do with the last naturally born humans in the universe!

This is the beginning of Book II

in the Saving Gaia Series. Stay tuned.

The mission to save humanity
has just begun!